Keeper of
the Universe

Andra
Calling B for Butterfly
Moonwind
Star Lord
The Warriors of Taan
Children of the Dust

Keeper of the Universe

by LOUISE LAWRENCE

_____ **Clarion Books · New York** _____

Clarion Books
a Houghton Mifflin Company imprint
215 Park Avenue South, New York, NY 10003
Text copyright © 1992 by Louise Lawrence

First published in 1992 under the title BEN-HARRAN'S CASTLE
by The Bodley Head Children's Books,
an imprint of the Random Century Group Ltd.,
20 Vauxhall Bridge Road, London SW1V 2SA ENGLAND

Printed in the U.S.A.

Library of Congress Cataloging-in-Publication Data

Lawrence, Louise, 1943–
[Ben-Harran's castle]
Keeper of the universe / by Louise Lawrence.
p.   cm.
Summary: Seventeen-year-old Christopher is kidnapped from Earth to
serve as a pawn for Ben-Harran, a renegade Galactic Controller, in
his fight against the Council of Atui and its policies of planetary
control.
ISBN 0-395-64340-6
[1. Science fiction.]   I. Title.
PZ7.L4367Ke   1992
[Fic]—dc20   92-2452   CIP   AC

BP   10   9   8   7   6   5   4   3   2   1

For Mo

LUCIFER

Angels are bright still, though the brightest fell.
But tell me, tell me, how do you know
he lost any of his brightness in the falling?
In the dark-blue depths, under layers and layers of darkness,
I see him move like the ruby, a gleam from within
of his own magnificence,
coming like the ruby in the invisible dark, glowing
with his own annunciation, towards us.

D. H. Lawrence

PROLOGUE

IN THE CORNER of a distant galaxy a world winked out. And in the huge observatory Maelyn watched it, a slow-motion replay of a death that should not have happened, an atmosphere burning, a consummation of fire. And the music altered. Vibrations of life shrieked and ceased, leaving only the soft, discordant murmuring of molecules, a crackle of static. On the scanners the swirling colors faded until nothing remained but dust amid a background of stars.

Maelyn clenched her fists.

"Ben-Harran?" she asked bitterly.

"Who else?" replied the operator.

"Was it Earth?"

"Zeeda," replied the operator.

Ice-blue anger blazed in Maelyn's eyes.

"He will be charged!" she said. "He will stand before the High Council of Atui and answer for this! Demotion was not enough, it seems, nor banishment neither. This time Ben-Harran must be condemned! For the destruction of a planet there can be no defense!"

She turned and left the room. And the Erg Unit followed

her, an antiquated robot that parodied the human form, programmed to serve, programmed to remember. Facts filled its computerized mind from a life a thousand years long, obsolete mostly, but occasionally useful.

"Ben-Harran is guilty of genocide," Maelyn informed it.

"Guilty," the Erg Unit repeated.

"He is responsible for the extinction of . . . how many species?"

"The planetary average is one billion, five hundred one million, two thousand twenty-six, mistress."

"And on Zeeda specifically?"

"Insufficient data, mistress."

"You mean you don't know?"

"In Atui, we have no access to Ben-Harran's evolutionary files."

"We have spies," Maelyn said curtly.

"Not in Ben-Harran's castle," droned the Erg Unit.

Maelyn frowned. Her white gown shimmered, and an aureole of light surrounded her.

"Why not?" she demanded.

"Disloyalty in a living organism is always detectable, mistress."

"And in a machine?"

"Insufficient data," repeated the Erg Unit.

Maelyn glanced at it.

She had been meaning to replace it for several decades.

"I think we should find out," she said briskly.

CHAPTER 1

CHRISTOPHER AWOKE with an earache and a pain in his head. Beyond the window the sunset flickered, shifting shades of crimson, rose and gold. The room was small, shadowy in the light, but he could see his guitar and suitcase standing in the corner, a single chair and the bed on which he was lying. He could not remember how he had gotten there.

He tried to think back. Heathrow, London's busy airport, in April, a week before Easter, rain on the runways and the plane five hours late taking off, bad weather over the Alps and an air controllers' strike. He had been going to Athens to work in a tourist hotel—serving drinks, clearing tables, mopping floors. A damned fool, the principal called him, opting out of his exams and throwing away his chances. And his parents were furious. He should go to college, study economics or business management, aim for a well-paid job and a decent career, they said. It was as if life's only purpose was the getting and spending of money. Airborne in a rush of darkness, Christopher felt he had escaped from something.

He remembered ham salad and custard served on a plastic tray, music playing through headphones, distant lightning seen through the porthole window. The plane had shuddered as it hit the storm front. It was nothing to worry about, the captain said. Flight attendants served drinks, and a woman wearing a pink dress headed for the lavatory.

Then . . .

Christopher stopped. He did not want to remember what happened next. But the image came unbidden into his head—a moment of shock, a flash of white light as the plane exploded, microseconds of knowing he was about to die, screams of terror before annihilation. And there his memory ended. After, it was nothing but blackness and stars, strange shifting dreams of a silver robot, a man robed in darkness, music he could not remember and could not forget. It was there in his mind and all around him, elusive and irresistible. If he closed his eyes, he would dissolve and become it, floating and formless and fleshless as air, his body gone, his human soul a song.

But the sky colors flickered.

And a sound disturbed him.

Someone opened the door and he turned his head. Nothing moved, yet someone or something was there, a rustle of dark, a black terrifying presence standing tall and motionless. The air seemed to crackle with infernal power. Then whoever it was withdrew and the door closed again, although something remained—the residue of an existence, the aura of a nightmare that was slow to fade, and Christopher's fear. His heart hammered and the room pulsed with blood-red light, as if the sky burned or the horizons were on fire. Not sunset, thought Christopher, but the fires of hell. He had died and gone to the Devil.

*　　*　　*

Dead people, however, did not suffer from earaches and pains in the head. Nor did Christopher believe in hell, or heaven. He concluded he must be alive, somewhere, somehow, miraculously survived. He felt his limbs beneath the bedclothes, all intact. He was uninjured, it seemed, apart from possible concussion; the gap in his memory, the pain in his brain. Beyond the window the sky flickered, shocking blue and phosphorescent green. Lightning, thought Christopher, a thunderstorm, dry, without rain. Unless it was neon signs above a city? He was in a hospital, perhaps, in Rome or Milan, near to wherever the plane had crashed.

He searched for a bedside bell and failed to find one.

He called and no one came.

Then someone did.

The door opened again. A light was turned on and the outside sky was gone in reflections of stark white walls and a naked electric bulb hanging from the ceiling. Christopher blinked in the sudden brightness. He was staring at a woman with wild brown hair, at a pair of yellow eyes that stared at him. She was not a nurse; more like a huntress or an Amazon warrior. Her arms and thighs were bare and bronzed by the weather, her short leather tunic stained with grease and blood. And she did not look particularly friendly.

"Who are you?" Christopher asked warily.

"Drink!" she said.

And she thrust a cup to his lips.

Christopher spat. "What is it?"

"A brew that revives, or so I'm told," the woman informed him.

"It's foul!" said Christopher.

"Just drink it!" said the woman.

"I'll see a doctor first," Christopher said obstinately.

"A doctor?" said the woman.

"Or whoever's in charge here," said Christopher.

"Of you," said the woman, "I'm in charge. And you had best do as I bid or worse it will be for both of us."

Her voice threatened, and her yellow eyes were savage and proud. Yet she was afraid of something.

"Who are you?" Christopher repeated.

"Mahri," she said. "Mahri's my name. I was Queen of my tribe on the High Plains until I came here. Men trembled when I spoke. Now I am held captive and expected to wait upon myself and you."

"I see," said Christopher.

She was obviously mad, suffering delusions of grandeur.

One of the inmates, perhaps?

Maybe this was not a hospital but a lunatic asylum!

"Where are the others?" asked Christopher.

"What others?" asked Mahri.

"The crew? The passengers? That woman in the pink dress? I can't be the only survivor. And someone has to be in charge here apart from you. Where are the rest of the staff?"

Mahri shook her head. "There are no staff," she said. "No one but you and me and that stupid tin-can machine Ben-Harran calls a robot."

Christopher stared at her. A robot, she said. He had dreamed of a robot, silver and tall with spindly limbs. But maybe he had not been dreaming and nor was Mahri mad.

"Who's Ben-Harran?" he asked her.

Nervousness flickered in her eyes.

She glanced toward the door.

"Better not ask," she whispered. "He's a devil! A sorcerer! I know not what! Against my will I am made to serve him, housed like a pig and fed on crusts. But not for long!"

She leaned closer. Christopher smelled her breath, saw something crawling in her hair; and the pores of her skin were ingrained with dirt. Where did she come from? he wondered. Where, with her unkempt clothes, the knife at her belt and her fierce yellow eyes? He had watched her lips move, heard her speak an unknown language in a foreign tongue, yet somehow he understood.

"Drink!" she said. "Drink before the brew grows cold. I'll gather provisions and wait downstairs. We'll escape together. You can be my personal servant, carry my weapons and sleep outside my tent."

She was serious, thought Christopher. She was actually serious, expecting him to go with her and accept her offer of servitude. She *had* to be crazy.

"No thanks," he told her.

"You will refuse me?" asked Mahri.

"I'm not feeling well enough to travel," said Christopher. "I think I'd better stay here in the hospital."

Mahri stared at him . . . and then she laughed. It was a manic laugh, humorless and wild. Outside, the sky flashed violent blue and sheets of emerald, dimming the light. And her voice came pitying him.

"You'll learn," she said. "You'll learn just as I did. Better if I had stayed where I fell on the battlefield and died of my wounds than come here. This is no hospice of healing, boy. This is Ben-Harran's castle."

*   *   *

The brew cleared Christopher's head, and when Mahri had gone he tried to reason. Ben-Harran was an Arab-sounding name. He was a sheik, perhaps, and the plane had been blown off course, crash-landed in Syria or Azerbaijan.

Beyond the window the sky shimmered gently in shades of mauve and amethyst, twilight above a desert now the dry storm had ended, seeming to confirm his theory. Unless he was dreaming and unable to wake?

He touched the wall, hard stucco, perfectly real. Impossible to dream that kind of solidity. Nor was he dreaming the ache in his ear and the tiny scar he could feel behind it. He had been operated on, he thought. And it was all real, actually happening . . . those fluttering colors, the power and presence that had entered his room, Ben-Harran's castle.

Ben-Harran was a sorcerer, Mahri had said.

And if I believe that I'm as mad as she is, Christopher murmured.

Am I?

Talking to yourself is the first sign, he answered himself.

So what's going on? How did I get here? Where the hell is Ben-Harran's castle? And what about that robot?

There was only one way to find out.

Christopher rose from the bed.

A stone floor was cold beneath his feet, and there was nothing wrong with him apart from the crumples in his clothes and a slight sensation of giddiness that swiftly passed—no burns, no bruises, not a mark. From a midair explosion of a Boeing 747 he had escaped unscathed, as if he had been teleported away along with his baggage. It was all there—his guitar and suitcase, his hand luggage and the paperback book he had been intending to read on the flight. Hand-written labels stated his identity and destination. How had his baggage gotten here? thought Christopher. Who had rescued it and rescued him?

I ought to be dead. "Am I?" he wondered.

He studied his face in the window, pale but alive, essentially unchanged. Then, suddenly, beyond his eyes the sky erupted, burned and flamed, scarlet, spectacular, with tongues of yellow and white. A volcano blowing its top . . . or so Christopher thought—until he looked out.

"Oh my God!"

He clutched at the sill to keep himself from falling, stunned by the shock of what he saw. It was beautiful, terrible, the whole sky hung with light, veils of color sweeping toward him from the depths of space. He gazed into misty clouds of yellow and white, bands of pink and crimson and scarlet, mauve and blue, swirls of emerald, millions of miles wide. It was a rainbow nebula spiralling around him, a great shimmering aurora reaching out and out. And within it he saw the vague yellow shapes of gigantic suns, stars slowly forming and great worlds rolling by.

Spellbound, he watched. He had no thought in his head, no awareness of time, no sense of himself, no questions anymore. Belief and disbelief were both suspended, his memory gone, past and future swept away. He and Earth, the whole human race and all its achievements, were reduced to nothingness, as insignificant as dust. He stood, a meaningless scrap of existence in the midst of creation, a microscopic, shivering thing confronted by the power of God.

Fear wiped him out.

He could not bear it . . .

his own smallness . . .

the immensity of what he saw.

He shifted his gaze from the sky to the land. Mountains were dark on the far horizon, jagged outcrops of rock eroded by wind and etched by fire. Nearer, a desert of blood-red sand lay desolate and lifeless. He was high above it. Directly below, the cliffs plunged down into a well of darkness, and ink-black shadows stretched before him on the sand . . . the shadow of a castle on a crag, with towers and turrets and crenellated walls. In Ben-Harran's castle, on some unknown planet, Christopher realized he was imprisoned.

*   *   *

He sat on the edge of the bed trying to decide what to do. He felt sick with his own emotions, and what lay beyond the door filled him with dread. Whatever Ben-Harran was, he was unlikely to be human. He remembered the nightmare presence that had visited him, the god-awful power. A devil, said Mahri. Yet Christopher was bound to face him.

Go on, he urged himself.

I can't.

To face what you fear is the death of fear.

But he's alien, isn't he? Some kind of monstrous entity.

Do you know that for sure?

No.

But the thought terrified.

Ben-Harran was unimaginable, totally unknown, and why Christopher was brought to his castle he could not begin to guess. But there must be a reason. He had not been transported halfway across the universe for nothing. Yet what use was he to a being as powerful as Ben-Harran?

He won't eat you, he assured himself.

How do I know? Christopher thought darkly.

Who in their right mind would travel billions of light years for a mere culinary item? he argued. *Anyway, Mahri's still in one piece. And if Ben-Harran wanted me dead, I wouldn't be alive now, would I?*

I guess not.

And you can hardly stay in this room for the rest of your life.

No.

His throat was dry, and fear of what he must do made him sweat. He put on sneakers, unpacked a clean T-shirt and forced himself to open the door. There was no one about, just a long corridor with oil lamps set in alcoves, dim pools of light and shadows between them, dark and disturbing. Chill air made him shiver. He returned for a sweater, then stepped out into the silence.

On either side of the corridor oak doors opened into empty rooms where gray dust muffled his footsteps and the only sound was the thump of his own heart. Through arched windows the nebula flickered. And at the end of the corridor a spiral stairway led down and up. Downstairs, Mahri was waiting. He heard a metallic crash, her curse in the silence, and chose to go up. Here was another corridor, another succession of empty rooms, and he might have believed the whole place was deserted. Yet, somewhere in the rambling keep, among high towers and drafty galleries, he sensed a presence.

His fear increased as he went higher. The shadows shifted as the oil lamps fluttered, their small flames bending in a current of cold air as if someone, somewhere, had just closed a door. And did he imagine, in the room above him, footsteps on the floor and a trace of music? He listened and the silence filled his head, preyed on his nerves. He continued upward.

At the top, a fire door barred his way.

EMERGENCY EXIT, it said.

It slid open before him and seemed like a doorway through time.

Christopher stared. Behind him was a medieval castle where Mahri talked of sorcery and the oil lamps flickered. Ahead, the corridor was electrically lit, carpeted green with stark white walls, centrally heated, air-conditioned, like any modern office block on Earth. And he did not imagine the music—he actually heard it—eerie and discordant but strangely beautiful against a background of soft synthesized sounds. He walked toward it and the EMERGENCY EXIT closed behind him with a quiet click.

Hard to tell where the music came from, left or right, near or far. It was everywhere, shifting and drifting, closing and receding, as if the sky sang through the walls around him. And another automatic door opened soundlessly as he stood before it.

It was someone's apartment. Room beyond room Christopher saw, through arches translucent with light, gleaming dimensions, and walls made of glass or air, art forms and furnishings fabulous and fine, shot-silk fabrics and a jade statuette on a squat-legged table, a roof garden beyond where flowers bloomed among ferns and trees and fountains. Through the ceiling he saw the sky, singing colors and slow suns forming, trailing their planets through the mists above his head. And the floor shone like water. If he entered the apartment, he would drown, dissolve into music and color and light, be lost in the only reality there was.

Fearing it, Christopher turned his back, walked on along the corridor. Another door opened. There, he stood on a threshold into darkness, a darkness so absolute that if he stepped, he feared, he would plunge and fall into a bottomless abyss. No music here, just a silence that petrified him, paralyzed him, turned him deaf and blind. Yet somehow he perceived. Maybe his eyes adjusted or his mind saw a vast room full of metallic gleams, dials and switches and computer screens. And a swivel chair where someone was sitting.

A shape in the darkness swung suddenly to face him, a black undefinable presence that rose and became a man. Mighty spaces lay between him and Christopher, a black infinity that nothing could cross. Or maybe *he* could. Light grew around him, red shot with gold, a gleaming flickering aura, and his black robes rustled as he moved. Dark eyes glittered and his teeth flashed white as he smiled.

"Come in," Ben-Harran said softly.

Just a single step, into the darkness and his own fear, was all Christopher needed to make to meet Ben-Harran. Instead, he turned to run. But coming toward him along the corridor, swift and menacing, was the silver robot. An eight-foot-high torso, clattering metal feet and crimson eyes that flashed like warning signs above a highway, bore down on him. He did not wait to estimate its speed. At an even greater speed he headed for the EMERGENCY EXIT. The robot's voice called after him in stentorian monotones.

"Stop! Wait! Stay where you are!"

Then, between it and Christopher, the door slid shut.

*   *   *

Halfway down the spiral stairs he heard the robot following. The obvious place to hide was in one of the empty rooms so he slammed the doors as he passed, returned to his own room and wedged the chair beneath the handle. Metal feet clomped along the corridor above, but he knew the robot would find him eventually.

Meanwhile, he had gained a breathing space, time to think, to get a grip on himself. But his thoughts were hardly rational

—a kind of chaos in his head—and the chaos of the nebula swirled beyond the window, hellfire colors, gold and scarlet and vermilion. Upstairs in Ben-Harran's apartment he had heard the colors singing—shades that were music, or music that was substance, as if solidity were an illusion and everything he saw were nothing more than vibrations, shifts of the light and his own mind. He watched the great worlds rolling through the distances and he could not take it. He could not take the beauty and immensity, the terror he had felt in Ben-Harran's presence, all that had happened, the confusion in his head.

He had nothing to relate to, nothing in the sky or the desert land or in the castle where the robot hunted him. Only Mahri. And who was she? Some female Attila from another planet, probably. A warrior Queen, brought here as he had been for some unknown reason. Small wonder she seemed crazy, thought Christopher. No one could cope with this kind of transition, the loss of all that was familiar, all that was understood. He was trapped in an insane reality where the isolation appalled and terrified and there was no help, no appeal, no escape. All he had was himself, the dull awful ache of his own existence and an acoustic guitar.

He picked it up, sat on the edge of the bed and strummed a sequence of chords. The guitar sound comforted, as it always did. If he played long enough and loudly enough, he could forget who he was and where, lose himself in the rhythm of the music. His fingers moved skillfully across the strings, improvising a tune, a strumming of colors—the song of the nebula, red and gold. Contentment filled him.

Then came the knock at the door.

"Let me in!" called the robot.

The music stopped.

Awareness of his predicament came crashing back.

He saw the handle turn.

"Open!" said the robot. "I know you're in there."

Christopher retaliated, refused to be intimidated.

"Sod off!" he said.

There was a moment of silence.

"Illogical," said the robot. "Off is a preposition and cannot be sodden. Your command is meaningless."

"I mean . . . go away!" said Christopher.

"Conflicting orders cannot be obeyed. Firstly I must obey Ben-Harran. It is my duty to cater to the needs of all specimens brought to this castle."

"I'm not a blasted specimen! I'm a human being and I've got rights! Liberty is one of them. I demand to be set free."

"So open the door," the robot said logically.

"You must think I'm stupid!"

"Insufficient data. I cannot judge."

"Oh very funny!"

The door handle rattled and the chair shifted slightly as the robot pushed. With one swipe of its forearm it could have broken through, but it stayed where it was, outside in the corridor, its tinny voice calling through the crack. Christopher had no need to run from it or bar the door, it said. It was just an ordinary Erg Unit used for clerical, domestic and maintenance purposes, programmed to assist in whatever capacity.

Programmed by Ben-Harran, Christopher thought darkly. A towering hulk of sheet metal and computer circuits, brute strength without conscience or emotion, and totally loyal to its maker. Christopher, classed as a specimen, was not about to trust it.

"Go away!" he repeated.

"I must show you the kitchen," the Erg Unit said.

"I'm not hungry," Christopher informed it.

"All life specimens need regular sustenance."

Christopher ignored it, bent his head and strummed a melody on the guitar. Now electric blue and vivid green, the colors sang across the sky—and, once again, he tried to catch them—tones of music, tones of color, harmonizing as the Erg Unit went on chattering. But then he heard a different sound, a deep bass humming somewhere beneath him, like the turning on of some huge machine—a refrigeration unit or an electric generator, perhaps. The ground throbbed and the sound increased in pitch until the whole castle seemed to shake.

An earthquake, thought Christopher.

But somehow he sensed it was not.

Carrying the guitar, he walked to the window and looked out. And up from the darkness directly below, from the well of shadows at the base of the cliff on which the castle was built, the spaceship arose. It was domed and disc shaped, metallic black with flashing multicolored lights, lifting slowly to hover on a level with his eyes. And suddenly Christopher remembered.

He remembered ham salad served on a plastic tray.

A flicker of lightning seen through the porthole window.

A woman in a pink dress heading for the lavatory.

There had been a shape outside . . . something huge and dark hovering among the stars. Then the airplane exploded—a flash of white light—human screams. Ben-Harran was a devil all right! But he was not a sorcerer. The power he possessed was the power of science, and he used it to destroy. There had been three hundred passengers on board that plane. They must have died, all of them, blasted from the sky. Only Christopher had survived—survived to become a specimen in Ben-Harran's castle. A huge rage filled him.

"Why?" he howled.

But the ship veered away, curved upward to cleave a flight path through the nebula until it was lost from sight among the veils of colored light. And the chair gave way behind him, cracked and broke. He swung around in terror as the Erg Unit stepped through the wreckage. Camera-lens eyes gleamed redly as it approached, and Christopher did not stop to think. He swung the guitar, one almighty swipe of wood against metal, a twang of strings, a shower of glass and sparks. Struck in the face and caught off balance, the Erg Unit toppled, hit the floor with a deafening crash and sat there, silently, regarding Christopher through its one remaining eye.

"Oh no," it said weakly. "Not another! I am not programmed to handle aggressive natures. The woman attacks me whenever I appear, and now you! What have I done to deserve this?"

CHAPTER 2

IN ANOTHER GALAXY, above another world, the spaceship circled and cast its shadow. Then it veered away to land in the river fields beyond the town. It was one of the Overseers, Kysha supposed. Someone in the area must be showing signs of the Changes.

"I wonder who," she said to Elia.

"No one I know," Elia replied.

They returned to the house, to Elia's room, arranged the flowers they had picked and sewed some tapestry. Outside, the bright day changed. Clouds snatched away the sun. The room darkened and Kysha shivered in the sudden chill, put down her sewing and stepped onto the balcony.

"It's raining," she said in surprise.

"Don't be silly," said Elia.

"Come and see for yourself."

A few warm wet drops splattered on the leaves of the sun vine that coiled around the railings. Then the rain gathered momentum. Suddenly the air was full of it, a summer deluge beating on the roof, swilling along the overhead gutter and chuckling down the drain. Trees dripped in all the riverside gardens, and bruised flowers released their scents. And the river itself was pockmarked and pale.

"How strange," murmured Kysha.

Elia shrugged.

"There must be something wrong with the weather-control satellites," she said.

"It's never happened before," said Kysha.

"And who's that?" asked Elia.

Kysha looked where she pointed.

The men who loaded and unloaded the barges were gone, but someone walked along the towpath, a stranger wearing black garb who paused to look up at them.

"He must have come from the spaceship," said Elia.

"The Overseers wear white," said Kysha.

"Then who is he? And why is he staring?"

"I don't know," said Kysha.

She could feel his gaze, dark and disturbing, fixed on her face as if he were seeing inside her, reading her mind. Odd thoughts fluttered to the surface. She knew what she could not have known—that he had been searching all the towns and villages of Erinos, and now he had found her.

Fear lurched in her stomach.

"He's staring at *you*," said Elia.

"It's a free world," Kysha said nervously.

"So who is he? And what does he want?"

"I don't know," said Kysha. "And I don't want to know. Let's go inside."

Elia stared at her with sharp blue eyes.

"You're afraid," she said accusingly.

"What if I am?" said Kysha.

"Fear is a symptom of the Changes," said Elia. "You can't feel fear unless you're guilty of something. You must have broken the Life Laws, Kysha, and he's come to take you away."

Elia was teasing—Kysha knew that. But if she was capable of feeling fear, then she might be capable of feeling other unwholesome things. Maybe she had begun the Changes without knowing it? The thought worried her, nagged at her mind. She grew quiet and uncommunicative. And that was another symptom, Elia said.

"I wish you'd shut up," said Kysha.

"So's irritability and reversion to childish language."

"You had better report me, then!"

Elia laughed.

"Don't be silly," she replied.

*   *   *

Kysha left Elia's house when the rain stopped, shut the white garden gate and waved. Massed clouds made a premature darkness although the town was lit by gleams of watery sun, small houses straggling up the hillside, their walls startlingly white. From the quayside, loaded barges moved seaward, but Kysha walked in the other direction, along the towpath toward the bridge and the flight of steps that led up to the road. Dark arches brooded on their own reflections, and the river ran brown and full, almost in flood. Rowboats strained at their moorings, and flowers overhung the garden walls in damp, velvety colors.

She had walked that way hundreds of times before, but suddenly it was different. She saw with altered eyes everything shining with its own inner light—trees, river weed, the old stones of the bridge and the cobbles under her feet. And on the opposite bank, between clumps of willows, the meadow grass seemed unbearably bright, not green but golden. Something had been added to herself or the world, a quality magical and intimidating. The river was full of a power she did not understand. Willow leaves rustled in her mind, and the flowers possessed a potency of existence that was beautiful and scary. They were too much alive—blue skybells, red heartsbane, yellow sun vine. She would not dare to pick them. Yet she had, only an hour or so ago, she and Elia arranging them in a vase on the table.

Now they were changed.

Or she was.

No, thought Kysha. Something was making it happen—the wetness of rain and the slants of sun causing the light and life to shine from things, or someone influencing her eyes and her mind. She stared around. And there, ahead of her where the towpath passed beneath the first dark arch of the bridge, someone stood. She recognized him immediately, his black garb, his strange penetrating gaze. He must have been waiting all afternoon for her to come . . . and somewhere, in the fields now dark with shadow and hidden by cloud, a spaceship was parked. He had come to take her away, Elia had said.

Kysha's fear returned, and she whirled and fled. It had nothing to do with the Changes. Her footsteps beat on the cobbles, echoed across the quay and up the alley beside the warehouse, on up the street toward the town square. Shopkeepers closing their shutters for the night turned to stare at her, and a group of market traders sitting on benches outside the tavern jumped up in alarm. She had only to ask and they would protect her, and any house she entered would give her shelter.

She glanced behind.

She slowed—and stopped.

There was no sign of the black-garbed stranger . . . just shadowy streets, the river gorge dissolving into darkness and a sky turned the color of ink where sea gulls sailed on white wings and sheet lightning flickered.

It was stupid to fear, thought Kysha. Nothing bad could ever happen on Erinos—the Overseers would see to that. But clearly something was wrong. A spaceship had landed, and others whined unseen through the clouds overhead. They were searching, she thought, for a fault in the weather-control satellites . . . or searching for her, knowing she had changed. Had she? she wondered. And could she, against her will, without being aware of it?

"Don't be silly," Elia had said.

But the group of market traders came toward her.

"Is all well with you, young lady?"

"Yes," Kysha said breathlessly.

"You seemed afeared of something."

"I'm all right, truly."

They smiled and nodded.

"It's the weather," they said.

"A change in barometric pressure."

"Positive ions affecting people."

"The Overseers have announced it on television."

"There's a thunderstorm brewing."

"You'd best hurry home, my dear."

"Or stay here in town for the night."

"I'll go," said Kysha. "It's only a mile or so."

"Yes," said the traders. "And no need to be afraid."

Relieved, Kysha ran on, past the fountains in the town square and the Council Building and on up the long hill. Her head ached and she sweated profusely, but it was only the weather affecting her, the air heavy and still. Behind her the sheet lightning flickered and the sky grew ominous, and cooking smells wafted from open windows with scraps of laughter and soft conversations that excluded her. Suddenly she felt lonely—and that was another symptom of the Changes.

Why? she thought wretchedly.

What's happening to me?

Where the town ended, high walls surrounded the homes of the Changed Ones. Just for a moment, Kysha was tempted to pass through the wrought-iron gates, walk up the long drive and admit herself. Set apart and separated by their own experiences, the Changed Ones would understand how she felt, offer her counseling and advice. She knew them well enough . . . Arlon the Healer, Mistress Corrin and the other teachers at the school, Master Anders who preached the Life Laws. They were wise and kind, and she had no need to fear them.

Yet she did. If they suspected that she had begun the Changes, they would report her to the Overseers. She would be sent through the portal into the world of Atui, and when she returned, if she returned, she would be different, a Changed One herself, assuming a position of trust and authority . . . a healer, a teacher, a counselor or a judge. But people who rebelled against the Overseers never returned. They were transported away and were gone forever, absorbed into another dimension of existence. Atui was not to be feared, Mistress Corrin taught. It was simply a *parallel universe*, as real as the physical universe, as real as Erinos. But Kysha did not want to be exiled, banished from the place where she had been born and raised, separated from her family and friends.

She hurried away before someone saw her, on along the

open road between upland farms and stands of coppice. To left and right rutted cart tracks led to the scattered farms. Small lights winked a welcome, and she knew the lives of everyone who lived there, yet her loneliness increased, as if she no longer belonged in the land where she had been born but had become a stranger to it. She realized why. She carried a secret she could never share, a fear she could never reveal. By the thoughts in her own head she was separated just as surely as the Changed Ones. Behind her the darkness brooded, and in all the landscape nothing moved but herself.

*　　*　　*

Dev smiled as Kysha took her place at the table.

"Had a good day?" he asked her.

"Yes," she said.

But she lied, and was separated even from her brother.

You shall not lie, preached Master Anders. And whoever broke the Life Laws, whoever questioned or rebelled against them, could not be allowed to remain on Erinos. It was not a crime, taught Master Anders. It was a symptom of an altered state of awareness, a sign of intellectual growth, perhaps, or spiritual awakening. Those who witnessed changes in themselves or others should be glad, not ashamed. But Kysha was appalled. With a single falsehood she had sealed her fate.

She bit her lip, blinked back the tears, helped herself to cheese and salad vegetables and ate in silence. She was not brave enough to leave Erinos, travel with the Overseers and endure the loneliness of Atui. All she had ever wanted was here on the farm—the ordinary, natural changes of growth into womanhood, time and seasons—not some unimaginable ordeal in another dimension. And how could the Overseers know? she wondered. How, if she changed, could anyone know apart from herself? Her feelings were undetectable, and so was her lie. Dev had not noticed and neither had her parents. They discussed the storm that had yet to break, how it would damage the harvest, rot the hay and flatten the wheat. And in the corner of the room the television screen was no longer functioning. A fault in transmission, Kysha supposed. Impossible, she concluded, for the Overseers to find out about her. And anyway, why should they care?

"What's wrong with your food?" inquired her mother.

She looked up, startled.

"You're forgetting to eat," said Dev.

"I'm not very hungry," Kysha said quickly. "It's the weather, I expect. Positive ions can affect people, the Overseers said."

And it might be true, she thought.

The house seemed stifling, the lamps gone dim and the outside darkness seeping in through the open doors and windows. Sheet lightning flickered interminably, and no birds sang, no crickets churred. The only sound was the chink of cutlery on crockery and a soft patter of steps.

"Someone's out there!" Kysha said in alarm.

But it was only the milk goat crossing the yard. And later, the rustle of robes she thought she heard was no more than the wind through the vines. Her father frowned and closed the door.

"What are you afraid of?" he asked her.

"It's only a storm," said her mother.

"The Overseers have assured us there's nothing to get alarmed about," said Dev. "Don't you believe them?"

"Of course I believe them," Kysha said instantly.

"So what are you afraid of?" her father repeated.

"Surely it can't be a person?" said her mother.

"You can't be afraid of anyone on Erinos," said Dev.

"And if you are," said her father, "there must be something seriously awry with your thinking. Remember what Master Anders says—you should think no evil, for as you think, so shall you be."

Kysha might have confessed, but suddenly the curtains billowed inward and the storm broke. Thunder rumbled overhead. The farm dogs howled and sheer blue lightning forked down the sky. Then the lights went out and everyone forgot Kysha's fear. Her father fetched the oil lamps, Dev hunted for matches, and Kysha and her mother ran through the house to close the windows. Hard rain sluiced against the glass, drummed on the roof and swilled down the cart track outside. She gazed into a blur of darkness where trees tossed wildly beyond the barns. And did she imagine, in the next flash of lightning, a black-garbed stranger standing by the gate to the yard?

Kysha returned to the kitchen.

"Someone's out there," she said.

Lamplight flickered as they stared at her.

"Don't start that again," implored her father.

"We checked," said Dev. "And there was no one."

"And if there should be, he or she will be welcome in our house," said her mother. "Now stop this silliness, child. Sit on the stool and play us a tune on your flute."

Defeated, Kysha obeyed. She sat on the stool by the spinning wheel and began to play. Her parents' blue eyes smiled approvingly. It was a tune they knew, a melody taught at Mistress Corrin's school that Kysha had learned by heart. But the night sounds distracted her and she made mistakes, stopped to listen to the wind around the eaves and a soft tap-tapping at the door.

"What's that?" she asked nervously.

"Only the rain," said her father.

"Or the rattle of vine leaves," said Dev.

But Kysha saw a darkness move past the window.

The knock that came was loud and unmistakable.

"Don't let him in!" she screamed.

"Whatever's wrong?" asked Dev in alarm.

"Are you ill?" asked her mother. "Are you in pain?"

Kysha had no time to tell.

She cowered in the corner and the oil lamps guttered as her father opened the door. Then, in a rush of wind and rain and darkness, so tall he had to bend his head to enter, the stranger stepped inside. Behind him, the door closed again, and the room was filled with the blackness of his robes, the power of his presence. Like the night raging far away beyond the walls, Kysha was forgotten. Dev and her parents just stared and bowed as the stranger nodded a greeting.

His voice came softly.

"My name is Ben-Harran," he said.

*   *   *

Ben-Harran sat at the table, unwound the scarf from his face as Kysha watched him, unseen among the shadows, curiosity overcoming her fear. More than a mile he had walked from the town to the farm with the storm at its height, yet he was untouched by it, his clothes not even damp. She saw, dimly, the red flickering aura that surrounded him, saw the whiteness of his smile and the black glint of his eyes. He reminded her of a snake she had once seen on television, fascinating and dangerous, hypnotizing its prey. And all the power of the Overseers was nothing compared with Ben-Harran's, she thought. He could blot out the world with his anger, with a snap of his fingers turn flesh into stone or reduce Kysha to dust. But now, in the farm kitchen, he accepted a meal of bread and cheese as if he were no more than an ordinary guest.

Her father attended him.

"Will you take wine, Lord Ben-Harran?"

Ben-Harran smiled.

"I would not be caught drunk in charge of a spaceship," he said.

Dev laughed.

And in the dark corner by the spinning wheel, Kysha frowned. Drunkenness was overindulgence, Master Anders taught, and overindulgence was akin to greed, breaking the Life Laws. Yet Ben-Harran spoke as if he knew and had experienced such a state, as if he expected her father to ply him with liquor when all he offered was a single glass.

"Perhaps you would prefer milk?" said her mother.

"I would prefer to serve myself," Ben-Harran stated.

Her mother stood back.

Their deference annoyed him, almost, thought Kysha.

But Dev was bolder.

"You're not one of the Overseers," he declared.

"True," said Ben-Harran.

"So who are you, then?"

"I'm one of the Galactic Controllers," said Ben-Harran.

Dev whistled. "An Overseer of Overseers! That's important!"

"We are honored you should visit us," murmured Kysha's mother.

"And why are you here?" inquired her father.

There was a small silence, undisturbed by the rain that lashed the windowpane or the creak of the stool on which

Kysha sat. Her heart thudded in fear and anticipation, but Ben-Harran appeared not to notice her. His head was bent, his face in shadow, although the lamplight shone on the bare white walls of the room, on the shelves of terracotta pots and cast-iron saucepans, on the metal flute that lay discarded on the table. Slowly his long fingers reached for it and he picked it up, studied it thoughtfully. And his words fell like a death knell when he finally spoke.

"I'm here for Kysha," Ben-Harran said.

Fear turned to terror as Kysha rose from her stool, then ceased quite suddenly when Ben-Harran looked at her. A strange stillness took hold of her mind, a space in her being where emotion could not exist. The dark eyes glittered and held her and she understood. He was a Lord of the universe, a Controller of a galaxy. He dreamed the stars in their courses, engendered worlds, endowed substance with life. She was not obliged to go with him—yet if she would obey the Life Laws, she must also obey one who had created them, accompany him out of choice.

Ben-Harran nodded and pocketed her flute.

"I'll wait for you outside," he said.

Then his eyes released her and he was gone into the night. In the room the silence remained, lamplight flickering in the eyes of people Kysha might never see again. All her feelings came rushing back, mixing with theirs, her mother's tears, her father's pride and sadness and Dev's confusion.

"Oh my dear child," her father murmured.

"It's so sudden," wept her mother.

"Why didn't you tell us?" asked Dev. "Why didn't you tell us you had begun the Changes? We could have helped you. We could have come with you to Master Anders, shared what you have been going through and prepared ourselves. It

should have been a gradual departure, something to cele-
brate and be glad about, not this awful unexpected leaving."

Kysha shook her head.

Everything welled up inside her.

And her voice was a shriek.

"It's not like that!" she cried. "Ben-Harran has made a
mistake! It's not me he wants, it's some other person. I
haven't changed and I don't want to leave Erinos. Tell him,
Father! He can wait out there forever, but I won't go with
him. I won't! I won't!"

"Oh my dear child," her father said again.

He took her hands in his and his voice was gentle, trying to
comfort her and explain. Galactic Controllers did not make
mistakes, he said. And if she was not aware of the Changes
now, then she soon would be. The process was irreversible,
and one day she would begin to despise the smallness of her
life and the ignorance of everyone around her. It would be a
terrible thing if she, as a grown woman with a husband and
children of her own, should then discover a need to fulfill
some inner potential and abandon them or sacrifice herself
because of it. It would be a source of too much unhappiness.

"To cause misery to yourself or others is a severe breach of
the Life Laws," said her father. "Inevitably the Overseers
will come for you then, so you had best go now with Lord
Ben-Harran. No doubt he will take you to Atui, and that is
nothing to fear."

"I'll pack your bags," said her mother.

"We'll miss you," said Dev.

"You don't understand!" wailed Kysha.

They did, perhaps, but not her position. They saw her fear
as symptomatic of the Changes and accepted, as she could
not, that she must go. They would not stand with her against

Ben-Harran, tell him to leave and have her stay. Unchanged themselves, they trusted him without question. Those who controlled the universe—like the Overseers of Erinos—did so for the good of all existence, plant forms, animal forms and people. They could never defy a Galactic Controller, they said.

Alone, Kysha stared at them—her mother, her father and Dev. Blue eyes, kind and sad, but equally determined, cast her out and showed no pity. There was nothing she could do and nothing she could say that would convince them. It was not she who had changed but something outside her in the world of Erinos, out in the wind and rain and darkness where Ben-Harran waited. It was he, thought Kysha, who had caused this to happen, Ben-Harran himself, wanting her for some unknown reason. Fear and grief and anger churned inside her as she put on her cloak, picked up her bags and went outside to face him.

CHAPTER 3

IN A FLUTTER OF ROBES and rainbow auras the High Council of Atui rose from their places and prepared to leave the courtroom, their array of robotic advice machines trailing behind them. It had been a long session. One by one Ben-Harran's followers had stood before them. Men and women, once loyal, had returned to Atui through the space-time interface or in the black ships of Ben-Harran's fleet, appalled by the outcome of his policies, the destruction of Zeeda that filled them with grief and remorse. There would be no need of any further punishment, Maelyn agreed. That world would burn in their consciences through all eternity.

"Damnation can wait for Ben-Harran himself," she declared.

"Excuse me," came a shrill voice from the nearby air. "It is inadvisable to anticipate the outcome of any future event. Damnation indicates guilt, which is not yet proven."

The Councillors chuckled.

And Maelyn turned abruptly to face the floating machine.

This was the Erg Unit's replacement, a Quantizing and Omni-Reasoning Module, shining in the all-pervading light.

Hovering on a level with her eyes, was a pulsating sphere of silver alloy bristling with video and audio antennae, retractable arms, probes and pincers, a single proboscis and a set of tripod legs.

The Quorm, according to its makers, had been pre-programmed with all available knowledge and, with its lightning responses, it would act as an accessory to Maelyn's thinking, an extension to her mind. But she doubted she would ever get used to it—its twittering and burbling, arguing and questioning and correcting her every mistake. She wanted to swat it like an irritating insect and only the presence of her fellow Councillors prevented her. Their voices murmured in passing.

"Your Quorm is an impressive machine."

"And it's quite right, of course."

"It does not do to make assumptions."

"Especially where Ben-Harran is concerned."

"He is a dangerous adversary."

"And genocide is a dangerous charge."

"He could well refute it."

Maelyn shrugged.

"What if he does? We have proof enough and witnesses aplenty. A world has been destroyed and he is responsible. No argument he brings to bear can sway us into believing him guiltless."

"Excuse me," chirruped the Quorm. "But you cannot know that for certain. The ethics of responsibility remain open to debate, and you are speaking from a prejudiced position. . . ."

"And you," Maelyn said furiously, "will go back into your box and be returned to your makers if you are not very careful!"

Again the Councillors chuckled.

But their amusement was unrecognized by the crowd of machines that bleeped and whistled and trilled, became a blather of robot voices all clamoring and complaining to their owners. The Quorm was only fulfilling its purpose, they said.

Finally, Lady Luanna held up her hand for silence. She was older than Maelyn, the wisdom of ages shining in the gray of her eyes, her green-gold aura more brilliant than the light. Her voice, which spoke for the High Council and would in the end pass judgment on Ben-Harran, was soft with caution.

"Do not let yourself be goaded, my dear. As our representative you will indeed be speaking from a prejudiced position. But we who remain on the High Council must, like your Quorm, be impartial. Heed it, Maelyn, and do not be tempted to respond with your emotions, or Ben-Harran in the courtroom may reduce you to a state of raging impotence and then walk free."

"You would not allow that," Maelyn said quietly.

"Perhaps not," admitted Luanna. "But then it would not be a legitimate victory but a moral defeat."

There were murmurs of agreement.

Maelyn bowed her head in assent and let them leave, listened to their voices fading along the corridor, then walked to the window and stood gazing down on the city shining golden beneath her. The wind, warm as summer on a three-dimensional world, shifted the white satin sheen of her gown and the moon-pale strands of her hair, carried the scent of the seasons, leaf fall and flowers, apple bloom and ice. She, it seemed, would be as much on trial as Ben-Harran, and just for a moment she longed to be gone, abandon her position with the High Council and make her escape to the woods or the meadows or the mountains, the infinite distances only a wish away.

Land beyond land, the realms of Atui called her. She knew she could travel forever and find no end to them—only the light growing whiter and ever more brilliant, the vibrations of existence becoming faster and finer until all things faded in the mists of a power source not even Maelyn could bear to know. But wherever she went, she would not escape the memory of Zeeda, the death fires burning and Ben-Harran black in her mind.

She shook her head determinedly. She had a duty to fulfill, the fate of Earth and Herra-Venda and several other planets to consider. Worlds that would be destroyed just as surely as Zeeda had been destroyed if they were left to Ben-Harran. No, thought Maelyn. She had a duty to bring him down.

She turned to face the courtroom where he and she would meet—whether he came of his own free will or was escorted by her Erg Unit and the white forces of Atui. Everything waited—the long table on the dais where the High Council would sit in judgment, the great arena of marbled floor and the rows of tiered seats beyond the arching columns. Empty now, they would fill with people and color, a massed audience to hear Ben-Harran defeated.

Maelyn stared.

High among the roof vaults she saw the Quorm, dipping and spinning in an aerial dance like a bumblebee in flight, as if it had neither thought nor care nor purpose.

Her voice echoed.

"Come down!"

But it was not the Quorm who answered her.

The intercom crackled.

"Lady Maelyn," announced the operator. "We have

received a report from our Overseers on Erinos. The satellite system is malfunctioning. As yet there is no suggestion of any adverse affect on the population, but a few moments ago a black ship was seen leaving orbit. Identification is uncertain but we suspect . . ."

"Ben-Harran!" Maelyn exclaimed.

"Excuse me," said the Quorm.

"You have no need to remind me that suspicion is not certainty," Maelyn informed it. "In this case, I am willing to wager I am right."

"Evens?" asked the Quorm.

"A thousand to one," Maelyn said curtly.

CHAPTER 4

THE ERG UNIT was damaged, blind in one eye, its visual functioning impaired. And with Ben-Harran away, it was in sole charge of the castle, a busy machine with endless duties to perform. It could have done without a physical attack on its person, it said. Christopher apologized, but it bore him no ill will, although it could not predict Ben-Harran's reactions and was not prepared to speculate. Diabolical punishments were left to Christopher's imagination, and his crime weighed heavily as he accompanied the Erg Unit down the spiral stairs toward the kitchen. Its footsteps clattered, metal on stone; but where the corridor began, the Erg Unit stopped. Something crashed in the distance and it turned in its tracks.

"The kitchen is along there," it said hurriedly. "The third door on the left. And Ben-Harran has left instructions that you may go wherever you wish within the castle apart from the main control room. Now, excuse me—I have to check the force field, maintain the life-support systems, mend the hangar door."

"Hang on," said Christopher.

"On is a preposition and cannot be . . ."

"I mean . . . wait a minute!"

But the Erg Unit had already departed, its metal feet clomping quickly back up the stairway, the echoes diminishing. A busy machine. Or was it a scared one? Christopher turned as Mahri emerged from the kitchen with a battle-axe in her hand. Patterns in ocher red adorned her face. Toothed necklaces jangled at her throat, and her eyes blazed yellow as wolves'. She might have lopped off the Erg Unit's head with a single swipe, but instead she saw Christopher and lowered her weapon.

"Oh, it's you," said Mahri. "What took you so long?"

"I met the tin-can robot," he replied.

Mahri spat. "I was not wrong then in thinking I heard its tread. But I am its equal in any contest of strength had it the guts to face me. I will protect you, boy, never fear."

"It's quite harmless," Christopher assured her.

"It is Ben-Harran's creature!" Mahri said viciously. "Spawned from his mind! Obeying his will! Now come with me. We shall escape from this place before Ben-Harran returns in his sky machine."

"Escape where?" asked Christopher.

"Anywhere," said Mahri. "Anywhere on Herra-Venda. We will put some distance between us and this castle, then head north to the High Plains and my own people."

She didn't have a clue, thought Christopher, no conception of where she was—light-years away from Herra-Venda, in a castle within a force field, on a desert world at the heart of a nebula. There was no way she could escape. And there was no way Christopher could explain the situation to her. Astrophysics would be meaningless to a barbarian queen with a war axe in her hand.

Reluctant to cross her, he followed her into the kitchen. It was a large dingy room, its ceiling beams draped with cobwebs, food scraps and ashes littering the flagstone floor. Above a smoldering fire hung a blackened cauldron, and around the walls dusty crocks stood upon dusty shelves, seemingly unused for centuries, and half a dozen battered chairs stood around a central table. And piled on the table was Mahri's baggage—a spear, a hunting knife and a great fur cloak made of sun-dried skins that smelled as odious as she.

Christopher wrinkled his nose. He saw a cockroach scuttle away beneath the baseboard, and a tap dripped stains into a cracked stone sink. Over it one barred window, gray with dust, admitted a little natural light. And did he imagine the nebula had ceased its flicker, changed into a solid sky?

Curious, he went to open the door.

"Stand clear," said Mahri. "I'll break it down."

"There's no need for that," said Christopher.

He drew back the bolts and stepped outside. The nebula was gone. Under wintry sunlight and a chill blue sky he stood in a concrete yard with garbage cans. High walls surrounded him, and a door in the corner led out again . . . into what?

"Herra-Venda," said Mahri.

"It can't be!" said Christopher.

"We shall soon be free. Go and fetch my things."

Christopher stared and made no move. Leaves of a creeper fluttered on the castle walls, purple veined with white, like nothing on Earth. And somewhere he heard a strange wild cry of an animal or bird. He did not understand how any of this could be. Here was a desert world, not Herra-Venda. Maybe it was an illusion, he thought, the sky an image reflected off the force field, the shivering leaves and distant cries no more than semblances of Mahri's home planet. But the apparent reality scared him, and so did she. No way was he going with her.

"I need to eat," he said.

Mahri stamped impatiently.

"There is nothing worth eating," she told him. "Nothing but stale bread and porridge. Rodent food! We will eat tonight, I promise you. I shall hunt and kill, and we shall feast on roasted meat. An atraxa, perhaps, or a young river bear. Now do as you are told. Fetch my things, and hurry!"

Christopher shrugged.

"All right," he said.

And he disappeared inside, escaped into the corridor and up the spiral stairs. His voice echoed as he called.

"Erg Unit! Where are you?"

*   *   *

There was no sign of the Erg Unit in the green-carpeted corridor, and the automated doors stayed closed when Christopher stood before them. Except for the door to the control room, which opened invitingly. What had been a threshold into darkness was now a blaze of light, a dazzling whiteness that had no source but seemed to come from the very air itself. It was like seeing through a mist to where distant walls shimmered and receded or were not really there at all. But the floor, when he stepped, seemed solid enough.

He could go anywhere in the castle except the main control room, Ben-Harran had said. And just for a moment Christopher hesitated. But not far away, on a central dais, were banks of computers luring him on. He settled himself comfortably in the great swivel chair and pondered things he did not understand—the power at his fingertips, dials and switches and video screens, digital keyboards that controlled and monitored God alone knew what. Maybe, if he touched, the entire castle would vanish and everything in it, or he might hear the nebula sing through the stacked amplifiers nearby, or maybe, somehow, he could contact Earth and let his parents know he was still alive.

OFF/ON.

He stared at the switch.

Shall I? he thought. But he was not that stupid, and somewhere he heard a noise like an elevator rising. Then, through the mists of light, a door opened and the Erg Unit emerged, eight towering feet of metal and component parts, programmed to serve Ben-Harran, and coming toward him. Its one red eye blazed in recognition, and caught where he should not have been, Christopher sprang to his feet.

"I haven't touched anything," he said hurriedly.

"Scrobbits," said the Erg Unit.

"Pardon?" said Christopher.

"Six twelve-millimeter scrobbits," said the Erg Unit.

"In reference to what?" asked Christopher.

"The hangar door," said the Erg Unit.

He watched curiously as the Erg Unit rummaged for parts in a drawer full of nuts and bolts, wires and wrenches. It seemed totally unperturbed that Christopher had disobeyed Ben-Harran's orders. Rules were made to be broken, it said. How else could individuals test their validity? True compliance was a matter of personal choice, and Ben-Harran did not demand it.

"Except from me," droned the Erg Unit. "A machine has to obey orders. Do this . . . do that . . . and I have no choice."

"I see," Christopher said dubiously.

But he knew he had not begun to see, not begun to

understand who Ben-Harran was or why he, Christopher, had been brought to his castle. And the Erg Unit knew nothing of motive or intention. Ben-Harran had not informed it, it said. Christopher was simply a specimen from Earth as Mahri was a specimen from Herra-Venda.

"Mahri thinks she's still on Herra-Venda," said Christopher.

"She is irrational," said the Erg Unit.

"Yes," said Christopher. "Well, that's one way of putting it. But it's not just her. She thinks we're on Herra-Venda, right? I know we're on a lifeless planet revolving around a star in a gaseous nebula. Yet when I opened the back door, I saw a blue overhead sky. So how do you explain that?"

"Illogical," said the Erg Unit.

"Quite," said Christopher. "But there must be an explanation. I don't believe it was real, but I did see it and I wasn't imagining. Is there some kind of machine in here that produces hologram images? I mean . . . what's all this computerized stuff for?"

With the scrobbits clutched in its hand the Erg Unit began to inform him, and Christopher wished he had never asked. It went on and on, long droning details of systems functioning, maintenance procedures for the castle's biosphere, the principles of dimensional displacement and psychomaterialization, photon amplification and space-time interface thresholds. It was all beyond him, too technical, too advanced. He just sensed the enormity of it.

"Hang on a minute," said Christopher.

The Erg Unit regarded him. "A minute is a division of time and immaterial. How can I hang on it?"

"I mean slow down."

"I am already stationary," the Erg Unit replied.

—— 42 ——

"So suspend your vocal functioning," said Christopher. "Or, in other words, shut your trap and let me think. What you're saying is all too complex for me to understand. Never mind the mechanics of the situation. Let's stick to what's relevant. Like where exactly are we? Why am I here? How did I get here? How long does Ben-Harran intend to keep me? And who the hell is he, anyway? Did he really blow up the plane I was on? Erg Unit? What's the matter?"

Something whirred and clicked in the Erg Unit's skull, a sound like an antique clock about to strike. Its one red eye flashed and pulsed, blazed brighter and brighter, blanked and went out. Scrobbits clattered on the floor as its thin metal arms fell limply to its sides. And there it stood, motionless, switched off inside, as if it were dead.

Christopher gazed at it in alarm. Minutes went by and it remained nonfunctioning, a busy machine with duties to perform, in sole charge of the castle. Without it, the surrounding force field could start to decay, the life-support systems falter and fail, the internal atmosphere seep out into space. Christopher thought the white light had darkened already and imagined a growing chill.

"Speak to me, Erg Unit," he begged.

Its eye glowed red as it switched itself on.

"Where am I?" it droned. "Why am I here? How long and who the hell? You hang on a minute, shut your trap. Where am I? Who the hell? I cannot compute. All systems overload. You slow down! Sod off! I am going to the basement to mend the hangar door. That's why I'm here. How long? Who can tell?"

It wandered away, dazed and muttering.

The elevator door closed behind it, and it was gone.

Christopher stared after it. It might be a phenomenally

clever machine, its data banks loaded with relevant facts, but it could not respond to a string of emotionally charged questions as if it were human. All systems overload, it said. If he wanted to learn anything of value from the Erg Unit, he had to learn how to extract the information—ask one question at a time, make sure it was logical, and allow time enough for the answer. Chastened, Christopher picked up the scrobbits from the floor and waited by the elevator to follow it.

*   *   *

He waited for the green illuminated arrow to go out as the elevator reached the bottom of the shaft, waited for the Erg Unit to alight, then pushed the call button and waited again for the elevator to rise. But before it arrived, he suddenly sensed something happening in the room behind him and turned his head. Over by the far wall, which might not be a wall at all, a square of misty air seemed to brighten, as if an unseen door had opened, letting through a yellower, much more brilliant light. Sunlight, thought Christopher, and within it he saw a shape slowly forming, a strange coalescence that glowed ghostly for a moment and then solidified into a human figure.

He saw through a barrier of glass or air a woman, tall and slender in a gown of satiny white, her waist-long hair the color of starlight on a winter's night. Beautiful and unearthly she appeared to Christopher, a being glowing with gold-white power, a radiance shining around her. He stared at her in awe, not knowing if she was really there or just an image made out of sheer air. Ice-blue eyes regarded him and, sweet and clear, her voice floated across the distance of the room.

"Who are you?" she said.

He bowed awkwardly. "My name's Christopher, lady."

"Named for the saint. You're from Earth, then?"

"England," said Christopher.

"What are you doing in Ben-Harran's castle? Is he forced to seek companionship of lesser beings now that the last of his followers have left him? Or are you the witness for his defense?"

Her voice was scathing.

Christopher stared at her, speechless and confused.

"Well? Have you nothing to say?" she asked him.

He spread his hands. "There's nothing I *can* say. Yesterday, or the day before, I was on a plane going to Athens. Then I woke up and found myself here. I'm a specimen, apparently, and like the laboratory rat, I'm not consulted. I don't know why I'm here. I don't know what's going on, who Ben-Harran is, or who you are either, for that matter."

The woman frowned. "I am Maelyn," she said. "From the High Council of Atui. And Ben-Harran is a destroyer of worlds. Are you telling me you have been abducted?"

"To all intents and purposes, yes I have," said Christopher. "And I suspect Ben-Harran blew up the plane on which I was traveling with three hundred people on board."

Maelyn stared at him. "You suspect?" she said.

"I saw his ship," said Christopher, "hovering outside the porthole window just before the explosion."

"And they are dead?" said Maelyn. "Three hundred people? He will answer for this along with everything else!"

"Can you help me?" asked Christopher. "Can you help me escape from this place before Ben-Harran returns? Can you send me home?"

Maelyn nodded. "Yes," she said. "I can send you home. Open the space-time barrier and let me through."

"How?" asked Christopher.

Gently, clearly, Maelyn explained.

And he did as she told him, went to the dais and searched for the controls, nervously following her instructions. OFF/ON. The far side of the room began to shimmer and dissolve.

In a few moments Maelyn would enter Ben-Harran's castle. But hard metal fingers gripped Christopher's wrist, and the Erg Unit reversed the process.

"What are you doing?" Maelyn said angrily.

"It is forbidden," the Erg Unit informed her.

"No, it is not forbidden," Maelyn retorted. "I command you, Erg Unit. Open the interface barrier and let me through!"

"All trafficking with Atui is forbidden, mistress."

Maelyn stared at it, a one-eyed machine.

"You have been reprogrammed!" she exclaimed. "A thousand years of loyalty have been erased! How did he know, Erg Unit? How did he know you were sent here to serve me?"

"Insufficient data," droned the Erg Unit.

"And where is he?" Maelyn asked bitterly. "Where is the devil who is now your master?"

"He is absent from the castle, mistress."

"I suppose, by some chance, he would not happen to be in the vicinity of Erinos?" Maelyn inquired. "Our Overseers report freak weather conditions and a total breakdown of the satellite-control system."

"Insufficient data," the Erg Unit repeated.

Maelyn shrugged. "Of course, he would be hardly likely to inform you. What you do not know you cannot tell, and we have yet to invent a machine that will lie for us. You delivered the charge, did you?"

"Yes, mistress."

"And does he accept it?"

"I know nothing of intention, mistress."

"Ah well," said Maelyn. "You will tell him I called, Erg Unit."

"The castle records all that takes place in it, mistress."

"Then I bid you good day," Maelyn said curtly.

"What about me?" asked Christopher.

Maelyn shook her head. "Right now," she said, "there is nothing I can do. You are Ben-Harran's creature and I have no jurisdiction in this matter. Your return to your home planet is dependent upon him, I'm afraid."

Then she was gone, her image fading in a blaze of gold-white light, returning to Atui from where she had come. A thousand questions whirled in Christopher's brain. Who was she? And where was Atui? What did she mean when she said Ben-Harran was a destroyer of worlds and Christopher was his creature? And if the Erg Unit had belonged to Maelyn before it belonged to Ben-Harran, then how much did it know? Metal fingers still gripped his wrist as he turned to it.

"Where's Atui?"

"Scrobbits," said the Erg Unit.

"Oh yes," said Christopher. "They're in my pocket."

*   *   *

Deep below the castle, a warren of tunnels had been hollowed from the cliff. Fluorescent strip lighting glowed eerily yellow, as if the power were running down, too feeble to alleviate the gloom or warm the air of the place. But Christopher was mostly oblivious to his surroundings, to cold or damp, pangs of hunger and the passage of time. There, in a disused underground control complex, among perished space suits, shower units without water, rooms full of welding gear, workbenches and mechanical parts, among wall screens and computers covered with dust, he questioned as the Erg Unit worked, his human voice echoing through the emptiness.

It was not an easy process. He had to remember, always, that he was dealing with a machine. It could not refuse to answer him, but it had no imagination, no intuition and a completely literal understanding. Far too often his questions were ambiguous or illogical, the Erg Unit unable to reply. Insufficient data, it said. Yet it was programmed to remember everything. Every detail of its own existence, all it had ever seen and heard both in Atui and in Ben-Harran's castle, was stored within the microchip circuits of its brain. And slowly, by precise questioning, it supplied the facts that Christopher pieced together.

Atui, it seemed, lay at the heart of the known universe. It was a world beyond the interface, nowhere and everywhere, a parallel universe that could be reached only by crossing the space-time threshold. And the High Council were administrators, Maelyn among them, a powerful personage. With the help of Galactic Controllers and Planetary Overseers, the High Council of Atui ruled every planet in the cosmos, said the Erg Unit.

"Nobody rules Earth," said Christopher.

"That is correct," agreed the Erg Unit.

"So you're talking gobbledygook, aren't you?"

The Erg Unit considered.

"No," it decided. "Gobbledygook is meaningless. I am programmed to speak logically on all occasions."

"But what you're saying is blatantly untrue!"

"A machine cannot lie," said the Erg Unit.

"But you've just told me that Atui rules every planet in the cosmos, and that's a false statement."

"Evolutionary programming is responsible for the presence of all life forms in the material universe, including those that exist on Earth," the Erg Unit informed him. "Elsewhere, the supervision of evolution remains constant, particularly the intellectual development of intelligent life forms. Their social and technological advancement is always controlled by the Planetary Overseers."

"But not on Earth?" asked Christopher.

"Not on Earth," the Erg Unit assured him.

"Why's that?"

"This galaxy is ruled by Ben-Harran," said the Erg Unit. "He does not employ Planetary Overseers. All species are free to develop according to their natures and are responsible for their own actions. No controls are imposed on the human populations of Earth or Herra-Venda or any other planet. Excuse me. . . ."

The Erg Unit went clattering along the corridor to the main hangar. Standing on the edge of it, Christopher felt dwarfed by its size, the opposite walls too far away to see and the roof so high above his head, it vanished into darkness. Dull lights hung suspended, and out on the vast expanse of crumbling concrete could have been parked a dozen ships or more. He tried to imagine it brilliant with power and light, ringing with noise and the bustle of men, spacecraft arriving and departing.

"What went on here?" he asked. "Some kind of galactic war?"

His words were drowned in a rumble of sound, the slow terrifying opening of the hangar doors. Pulley chains rattled above him, chunks of loose concrete danced in the vibrations and the whole castle seemed to shake. Christopher expected the roof to crash down on him, expected to die as the air was sucked through the gap. But the doors opened and he stayed alive and the light of the nebula came flooding in . . . jade green, emerald and blue . . . great waves of color reducing him to the size of an ant.

An invisible force field protected Christopher and Ben-Harran's castle. And what kind of power did it take to build a place such as this? What kind of power to maintain it? Even now it confounded him, derelict and decaying, emptied of life, its electrical systems failing, its doors malfunctioning. They jammed half open, closed and jammed and closed again.

"It must be the gyrobalancer," the Erg Unit muttered.

Christopher followed it to the disused control room.

"The whole idea's monstrous!" he said.

"Pass me the wrench," said the Erg Unit.

"No beings, however benign, have the right to interfere in the lives of others. It's a total denial of individual freedom!"

"That is Ben-Harran's opinion," said the Erg Unit.

"He's not in cahoots with Atui, then?"

"There was a rebellion," said the Erg Unit.

"So that's what this place was for!"

"Ben-Harran's headquarters," said the Erg Unit.

"So what happened?" asked Christopher.

Once long ago, the Erg Unit said, Ben-Harran had been a member of the High Council of Atui. Then a rift had developed, two irreconcilable principles of freedom and control. Atui believed control was necessary and Ben-Harran rebelled. He was brought to trial and convicted on three main counts: failure to comply with established practices, incitement to revolution and the promotion of anarchy. He was demoted to Galactic Controller and exiled, along with his followers, to this world in the nebula where Christopher now was.

"What happened to the followers?" asked Christopher.

"They have returned to Atui," the Erg Unit said.

"Why?" asked Christopher.

"I know nothing of motive or intention," said the Erg Unit.

"Something must have happened to cause them to desert Ben-Harran."

"Ben-Harran is responsible for the destruction of the planet Zeeda," the Erg Unit said. "He is guilty of genocide, for the death of a world and the extinction of all species that dwelled on it. He will be tried before the High Council and condemned. There can be no defense."

Christopher stared at the Erg Unit in horror. For a while, despite Maelyn's gold-white beauty, he had believed Ben-Harran was right to defy the High Council of Atui and right to rebel. He had become a freedom fighter on a grand scale. But there were freedom fighters on Earth too, terrorists mostly, and however much sympathy Christopher might have for their causes, he could not condone their methods. There was no crime they would not commit—mass murder, blowing up aircraft, taking hostages—just like Ben-Harran, it seemed. But Ben-Harran had powers undreamed of on Earth and had destroyed a world. Memories moved in Christopher's mind, a being in the darkness with blood-red mists gathering about, the undispelled terror standing in the doorway of his room.

He had to get out of here, he thought.

And whether it was to Earth or to Atui made no difference.

He had to escape from Ben-Harran's castle.

*　　*　　*

Back in the main control room, in the warmth and light that shone as mist, where the computers waited and the Erg Unit monitored the life-support systems, Christopher made his plans. There was only one way out of Ben-Harran's castle, and that was through the space-time barrier into Atui, where perhaps Maelyn would help him return to Earth. But the Erg Unit was programmed. His wrist bore bruises. It would stop him by force if it had to. Someone, he thought, would have to lure it away while he set the controls and made his run. Mahri with her war axe, perhaps, if she had not already gone wandering away into an illusion of a world she thought was Herra-Venda. But if she had, she could not have gone far. Within the limits of the force field Christopher was bound to find her.

"I'm hungry," he announced.

And that was true.

Since the meal on the plane, which might have been weeks ago, he had eaten nothing.

"May I go to the kitchen, Erg Unit?"

"You are free to go wherever you want . . ."

"I'll have egg and chips," said Christopher.

"You may have whatever you decide," said the Erg Unit.

"I can't cook."

"You must learn."

"I thought it was your duty to cater to the needs of all life specimens brought to this castle?" said Christopher. "And Mahri is vicious. I need you to accompany me."

Having calculated the odds, he thought it was logical that the Erg Unit would try to avoid Mahri, and no argument of Christopher's could persuade it. It seemed that he would have to persuade Mahri to come to the control room. He went alone down the spiral stairs and along the corridor where the oil lamps flickered. Third door on the left, he remembered. It was slightly ajar and Mahri was still in there.

And something was with her, monstrous and alive. He heard the crash of a chair, sounds of a struggle and ghastly squawking cries.

A few quick steps took Christopher into the kitchen, where he saw, strung up by its legs from a hook in the ceiling, a great flightless bird. It was the size of an ostrich but thick set and heavier, with stubby wings and a horned beak that stabbed ferociously as Mahri hauled on the rope. Her biceps bulged, but strong as she was, she could not hold the weight of it alone. Sensing Christopher behind her, she turned her head.

"Help me!" she commanded.

It was automatic. He took the strain, kept himself clear of the snapping beak and flapping wings, and hauled the thing higher. Its cries deafened him, and the rope burned his hands.

"Hurry up!" he shouted.

Evening sunlight flooded through the open door, shone on the blade of Mahri's knife as she struck. Bright blood flowed, and her eyes glowed with triumph. It was as if some power in her had come alive, altered her looks, altered her age, made her seem younger. She was almost beautiful in her savagery with her short leather tunic, her bare, bronzed thighs and brown disheveled hair. Lithe as a dancer, she kicked a bucket underneath to catch the blood that gushed from the bird's slashed throat. It died with a gurgle, and she had half plucked its breast before its flutterings ceased.

"I told you we should feast tonight on roast meat," she said.

The strain wrenched Christopher's arms, and the smell of blood made him feel sick.

"How much longer?" he groaned.

Mahri heaved the table underneath and hacked off the bird's head.

"Let him down gently," she said.

It landed with a thud, a mountainous carcass that would feed half a dozen people for at least a week. Christopher stared at it. Alive, it could have killed him with a single kick, ripped him open with its great curved talons or disemboweled him with its beak. He could not imagine how Mahri had managed to capture it singlehandedly, or where she had found it. It was called an atraxa, she told him. Outside was a whole flock of them, and she was as good a hunter as any man.

"I can't believe that!" said Christopher.

Across the body of the bird, Mahri stared at him, her yellow eyes blazing.

"Once," she said, "no one would have dared call me a liar! Nor would you now, boy, if you had known me then! You would have bowed before me or paid the price for your disrespect! And dead as the atraxa you will be if you do not watch your tongue! Besides, where is your gratitude? I have killed for you, that you may eat and regain your strength before we make our run. Now get plucking!"

Bewildered, wary, afraid to disobey, Christopher pulled at the toughened wing feathers. This bird was no illusion. And outside was a whole flock of them, Mahri had said. Black feathers flew. There was blood on his hands and the kitchen had turned into an abattoir, scented with death and chilled by the wind of a world that could not exist. A knife in the sunlight cut the vent, and hot stinking entrails came pouring out. It was all real—everything—the squelch—the smell.

Christopher gagged and ran for the door, across the yard

and through the gate to lean against the surrounding wall. No death out here. The wind whined cold around the ramparts of the castle, fluttered the leaves of the creeper, then clambered over its stones. And the castle's shadow fell long with the evening, stretching away over the grass plain of Herra-Venda that swept clear to the sky. Numbed out of thought, he stood and watched the flock of great dark birds grazing among patches of snow. Then, black and streamlined and streaking across the horizon, came Ben-Harran's ship heading home.

CHAPTER 5

K YSHA SAW THE PLANET loom through the mists ahead, a
dark disc among drifts of rainbow light. Nearer, and she
saw the surface features, rilles and craters and deserts of
dust, a world as barren as the moons of Erinos. Seated beside
her, Ben-Harran opened the communications channel, and a
robotic Erg Unit switched off the force field and let the ship
pass through. Emerald clouds swirled past the window and
vanished in a moment of black nothingness . . . and when
they emerged, the nebula was gone.

Kysha blinked in the bright sudden light of a nearby sun,
saw a solider sky of pale, cold blue and massed cumuli below.
And she glimpsed through breaks in the cloud what seemed
to be a different world beneath, a rugged plain where dark
creatures grazed, small as ants among pockets of melting
snow.

"Herra-Venda," Ben-Harran informed her.

"How?" she asked curiously. "Dimensional displacement?"

"Psychomaterialization," Ben-Harran said.

"So someone's mind is creating it?"

"You obviously understand the concept," Ben-Harran remarked.

"The Overseers taught us," said Kysha. "There was a series of television programs on the subject. And once, one of the Overseers visited the school. She manifested a flower out of thin air. It was quite real. We could see it, smell it, touch it. And as we think, so shall it be. But I have never seen a whole world become reality before."

"Then you have not seen Atui?" Ben-Harran inquired.

"No," said Kysha. "We all know of it, but we have not seen it. It exists in a parallel dimension, another universe in the mental plane. Nowhere and everywhere, the Changed Ones tell us. But they do not tell us what it is like, and the Overseers have not shown us."

"And you cannot envision it?"

"How can I envision what I don't know?" asked Kysha.

"And you know so much," Ben-Harran murmured. "Yet if you cannot imagine Atui, then all you know amounts to nothing at all."

Kysha was stung.

He made her feel small and ignorant, a worthless individual. And the feeling troubled her, unwholesome, unhealthy, assailing her against her will. On Erinos she had been taught that everyone mattered, but he undermined it, a lifetime of learning gone in a single second. She bit her lip. She was no longer afraid of him. Her fear had been of the future and was irrelevant now. She was quite safe with him. A Galactic Controller, for all his power, would inflict no harm. Yet in a few words, everything she was had been swept away, dismissed as insignificant, and again she wondered why Ben-Harran had chosen her.

She remembered the walk through the darkness, the warm

shelter of his aura where neither the wind nor the rain could touch her. Once she had accepted the inevitability of her departure, her grief had faded and she trusted him completely. She felt almost privileged to be beside him, elevated above all others, a special person. He had chosen her, he said, because she was perfect, a perfect representative of a socioevolutionary system, never questioning or rebelling or breaking the Life Laws. He said she had only to adhere to them, remain as she was, and he would return her to Erinos and vouch for her unchanged condition. She could pick up the threads of her life as if she had never been gone. But the Changes kept happening, feelings she did not want and did not like, coming to plague her. And did Ben-Harran know? she wondered.

She glanced at him.

Darkness glowed richly around him. She could feel it as a quality, deep and beautiful and awesome, burning with power and life. It was a terrible thing to realize that although he had chosen her above all others, she really meant nothing to him, no more than a bird in a cage or a bug in a jam jar, some kind of specimen. However kindly he treated her, however much attention he paid her, it was not because she was special but because she was there. The knowledge rankled, a mixture of anger and humiliation, unfamiliar feelings she had never learned to cope with, that now she had to struggle to suppress. She had to make him notice her, make him aware of her existence.

"My ear aches," she complained.

"It's the aftereffect of the language translator implant," Ben-Harran informed her.

"You assured me it wouldn't hurt."

"The ache will soon pass."

"I'm hungry, too," said Kysha.

"We land in a couple of minutes," said Ben-Harran.

"And who else is there?" asked Kysha.

He shrugged indifferently.

"A boy from Earth. A woman from Herra-Venda, Queen Mahri of the High Plains," said Ben-Harran. He laughed mockingly.

A queen, according to Kysha's understanding gained from the language translator implanted in her head, was an important person, an alien female dignitary who ruled over others as the Overseers ruled over Erinos. Yet Ben-Harran did not care about her either. Nor the boy, thought Kysha, whoever he was. And she would become one of them, three specimens from three different worlds.

Resentfully, she stared from the window as the ship dived downward to skim the horizon, watched as Herra-Venda faded, the grass going ghostly and flocks of great flightless birds turning substanceless as shadows. And this was Ben-Harran's world—rocks and sand and a castle perched on a crag, a rainbow nebula flickering around it.

He switched on the communicator.

"Open the hangar doors, Erg Unit. We're coming home."

*   *   *

Remembering Kysha's need, Ben-Harran led her down the spiral stairs and along a corridor toward the kitchen. Oil lamps in alcoves made pools of yellow light, but he was brighter, striding through red-gold mists, his mantle flowing blackly behind. And in his own castle he did not knock, just opened the door and bade her enter with a swift encircling gesture of his arm.

Kysha would never forget that moment. She recoiled in horror, whimpered, as Ben-Harran drew her protectively toward him. Still she saw . . . the mountain of flesh on the table, plucked and headless, that had once been a great living bird—the woman tearing at the corpse of it and the boy from Earth with his hands and clothes covered in gore. The vision was imprinted in her mind, blood and feathers everywhere, entrails stinking on the floor, the boy with his eyes brown as dung and his maggoty-white skin, and the woman, half naked, her thighs exposed, her yellow eyes shining as if she enjoyed what she did. They had killed a sensate creature, killed it deliberately, and violated its body.

Gently Ben-Harran held her, his darkness cradling her in a calm so deep she thought she would drown. But she could not forget what she had seen. It was a violation of herself as well, a brutal, diabolical act, thrust into her consciousness. And Ben-Harran had failed to shield her from it, brought her there and allowed her to witness what the Overseers of Erinos never would—human corruption worse than any-thing that existed in the animal kingdom. Angrily she pulled herself free from him and froze into her own aloneness.

For the space of one held breath no one spoke. Black, unexpressed rage hurtled outward above Kysha's head, and like a snake, Ben-Harran held them transfixed amid the mess of death, woman and boy with terror in their eyes. Dark feathers fluttered in a draft and there was no place to hide from the anger that had yet to break.

His voice was icy.

"There is a stink in here of rotten souls," he said.

"It wasn't me," the boy said hurriedly.

Proudly the woman tossed her head.

"It is a gutless wimp who is willing to stomach the meat but can't stomach the killing!" she retorted.

Kysha stared at her in revulsion.

"Are they carnivores?" she asked Ben-Harran.

Guiltily the boy chewed his lip.

But the woman was unashamed.

"You kill, you eat. And that is natural!" she announced.

"Is it?" Ben-Harran said softly. "Maybe to a leopard it is natural. But you are a human being and you have a choice. You shall not kill, Mahri. Have you heard of that commandment?"

It was the first of the Life Laws.

Kysha had learned it when she was three years old. She had stamped on a beetle and her father had chastised her. She could still remember the lash of his tongue, the lingering hurt, the unbearable no-love feeling she had suffered afterward. You shall not kill, he had said. That had been her only experience of punishment, and she had learned her lesson. Now they would learn, just as she had, and Ben-Harran would punish them. She saw the boy's face grow paler with the knowledge. But Mahri remained indifferent, turned her back, picked up the knife and hacked at the tendon of a leg.

"Priest talk!" she spat. "No one who lives in a world of men can heed the laws of God. It is kill or be killed on Herra-Venda. And what use is a bird if not for the table? I have no time for holy commandments, sorcerer. They are lip service, even among priests!"

Ben-Harran's black eyes glittered dangerously.

"How about you?" he asked.

The boy shook his head speechlessly.

And Kysha waited.

They would be punished terribly.

And she was glad!

"So be it," Ben-Harran murmured.

He drew himself up.

The air crackled and darkened and the mists grew around

him, magnificent and burning. The boy cringed, cried out a warning as blue bolts of lightning flashed from Ben-Harran's fingertips. Too late, Mahri turned her head, screamed as the lightning struck and the knife flew from her hand with a clatter of metal on stone.

She backed away. And the kitchen grew wild with wind; a chaos of feathers whipped into the air and whirled down the shafts of light that poured from Ben-Harran's raised hands. The carcass glowed blue. Entrails rose from the floor and reentered it. Blood spouts spiraled from the bucket. Head and claws and scraps of flesh flew and converged and reassembled into a bird among a pulsing sphere of radiance. And it moved, stirred, stood, massive and alive, leaped with a ghastly cry and fled after Mahri, through the open door, with a flutter of stubby wings.

In the silence Ben-Harran lowered his arms.

A few small downy feathers settled amid the dust.

And sunlight filtered through a grimy windowpane.

"Will it kill her?" asked Kysha.

"Do you wish it to?" Ben-Harran asked.

"It's what she deserves!" Kysha said hotly.

"Death?" said Ben-Harran. "For an error in understanding? Is that what they teach you on Erinos?"

"Murder doesn't happen on Erinos!" Kysha said bitterly.

The Galactic Controller shrugged.

"Why don't you go outside?" he suggested. "Across the yard is a gate that leads to a garden. In it you may gather all the food you need. And you go with her!" he told the boy.

*   *   *

Dismissed, Kysha crossed the yard. The nebula was gone in a blue overhead sky, and warm air brushed her face, psycho-materialized like the creeper that grew on the castle wall. It was unfamiliar, with star-shaped leaves, not of Erinos, not of her mind. It must be from Earth, she thought, from the boy's imagination, and likely the garden would be too. She opened the gate, and the strange, alien beauty took her breath away. Here were flowers such as she had never dreamed of, trees bearing scented blossoms and a feast of fruit, huge succulent vegetables and a bird singing sweetly on a bush.

"A blackbird!" said the boy. "I don't believe it!"

"I suppose you will eat it!" said Kysha.

"Why should I do that?" asked the boy.

"It's an obvious deduction, isn't it?" said Kysha. "There's no difference between that bird and the other except for its size. And are you a cannibal too?"

The boy stared at her.

And she stared at him.

He was repugnant, she thought.

And his pale face flushed with embarrassment.

"Of course I'm not," he said awkwardly.

"Why?" she asked him. "It's all meat, isn't it? All flesh? A bird or a beast or your own kind—there's no distinction."

"Yes there is," he argued.

"Not the way I see it," Kysha said cuttingly.

She marched away up the garden path, not wishing to be near him. How odd, she thought, that a garden so beautiful should spring from so vile a mind. Massed flowers were everywhere, their blooms bigger, brighter, more sweetly scented than any growing on Erinos. Kysha could never have imagined those stiff yellow trumpet flowers into existence, or dreamed the peachy fruits that grew against the wall. It was nature improved upon everywhere she looked—the clambering beans, the gourds and buds and seed pods, the huge scarlet berries growing on the ground among crowns of leaves.

"Strawberries!" exclaimed the boy.

"Are they edible?" asked Kysha.

"They are if they're real," he replied.

"Why shouldn't they be real?" asked Kysha. "What comes from the mental dimension is as real and existing as anything produced physically through slow growth. You ought to know that. You killed the bird that Mahri created!"

Christopher stared at her, not understanding what she said.

"Permission to eat?" he asked.

She watched as he glutted.

He reminded her of a hog she had once seen in a television program, mindlessly gobbling in the wild woods of Erinos. The boy was irreverent, ungrateful, unaware of the sunlight, the sweetness, the soil in its giving; he just crammed his mouth with whatever the garden provided—slim orange taproots, green seeds from fat pods, purple fruits torn from a tree. He had had nothing to eat since coming to Ben-Harran's castle, he said.

Kysha moved away, not wanting to know. She found a bush bearing nuts in a shady corner, gathered a handful and sat on a patch of grass to crack them with her teeth. Honey flies buzzed around crimson thorn flowers growing by the wall, and the blackbird sang for her, music in sunlight, softening the memory of death, sweet fluting notes that ended in a shrill cry of alarm. She heard footsteps on the gravel path and saw the boy's shadow fall darkly before her.

"My name's Christopher," he said.

"And I'm Kysha," she told him. "Now go away!"

But he sat on the grass beside her.

"Are you from Atui?" he asked.

"Erinos," Kysha said stiffly.

"So he *was* there!"

"Who?" she asked.

"Ben-Harran," said Christopher. "Were you abducted too?"

"Don't be stupid!" said Kysha. "Things like that don't happen on Erinos. Ben-Harran invited me, and I came of my own choice."

Christopher glanced at her.

"I'm sorry," he said. "There's so much I don't understand but I'd like to. If we could be friends . . ."

Kysha spat out the nutshell.

"After what I witnessed in the kitchen and knowing what you are, how can you possibly expect me to want to be friends with you? You're an assault to everything I believe in. You kill to eat and break the most sacred Life Law of all. Go away and leave me alone!"

Christopher made no attempt to go.

He sat motionless, staring across the garden.

His voice when he spoke to her sounded distressed and miserable.

"I'm sorry," he repeated. "I wouldn't have done it if I'd known, but I just didn't think."

"Ignorance is no excuse," Kysha said curtly.

He bent his head, pulled at the grasses that grew beside him, then squashed the ants that scuttled between them.

"You're doing it again!" raged Kysha. "Those are living things! Creatures that have a right to live! Can't you understand that?"

Christopher sighed. "I can't understand anything," he said. "I can't understand how any of this can even be." He nodded to the garden. "Nuts and strawberries and daffodils all in the same season. And not long ago it was Herra-Venda. I saw snow on the grass and atraxa birds grazing. And you and Mahri come from different planets. I watch your lips move, hear you speaking an unknown language, yet I know what you're saying. How?"

Kysha gazed at him in a moment of pity.

"Haven't you been educated?" she asked him. "Don't you have schools on your world?"

"Of course we do!" said Christopher.

"Then what are you taught?"

"How to get a job," said Christopher.

Kysha did not understand. She just knew he was ignorant.

"It's quite easy," she told him. "Thought is the greatest creative power in the universe. As you think, so shall it be. This garden is an image from your own mind, and in Ben-Harran's control room is a psychomaterialization stabilizer that makes it manifest. And the reason you understand what I'm saying and I understand what you're saying is because we both have a multilingual translator implanted at the base of the optic nerve."

Christopher felt for the scar behind his ear.

"You mean Ben-Harran put something in my head? Operated on me without my permission?"

"It's necessary, unless you're a telepath," said Kysha.

"You find it acceptable then? Whatever he does?"

"He's a Galactic Controller," said Kysha. "He knows what he's doing, and whatever he does will be justified."

"Justified?" said Christopher. "How can it be justified to make incisions in my head? Transport me here without a by your leave? Blow up a plane with three hundred people on board and destroy a planet?"

Kysha's hatred of Christopher was instantly renewed.

"Don't be stupid!" she said. "Ben-Harran wouldn't destroy a dog's flea, let alone a planet!"

"What do you know about him?" Christopher retorted.

"He's a Galactic Controller!" Kysha repeated. "And I don't need to know!"

"You haven't heard about the rebellion in Atui, then?"

"What rebellion?"

Christopher told her.

He told her about Maelyn and the High Council and how the universe was controlled. He told her of the conflict, the two opposing principles of freedom and nonfreedom. On Erinos, he said, no one was free because they were all part of a socio-evolutionary program imposed by the Overseers. But Ben-Harran had refused to participate, instigated a rebellion, lost his place on the High Council and been exiled from Atui along with his followers. And now he was alone in the castle, abandoned by all those who had once been loyal to him.

"He's a galactic terrorist!" said Christopher. "He's responsible for destroying a planet named Zeeda and the extinction of all species that dwelled on it. He's guilty of genocide, the Erg Unit told me. He's due to go on trial before the High Council and there's no defense. He's evil, Kysha. Powerful and evil. There's no knowing what he'll do . . . and we're stuck with him!"

Kysha scrambled to her feet.

Thoughts whirled in her head, everything Christopher had said, a muddle of mistaken facts. She knew about Atui and the Overseers and the socioevolutionary program of which Erinos was a part. There was nothing wrong with it. Nothing wrong with living in a controlled environment and obeying the Life Laws. Without the weather-control satellites they would all become prey to the elements, and prey to their own base natures without the Life Laws—just as Christopher was. You shall think no evil, the Life Laws said, but Christopher not only thought it, he spoke it and accused Ben-Harran. What kind of mind did he have? thought Kysha. What kind of hideous, twisted mentality?

"It's you who are evil!" said Kysha. "And I shall tell Ben-Harran! I shall tell him everything you've said! And as you've already damaged his Erg Unit, he's not going to like you very much."

She turned and marched away along the path.

And the sunlight darkened.

The sky began to flicker.

Monstrous shadows grew as the garden faded.

*   *   *

Kysha left Christopher in a desert, alone among rocks and sand, beneath a fluttering rainbow sky. She returned to the castle, and whether or not he followed she neither knew nor cared. Closing the yard gate behind her, she entered the kitchen.

The Erg Unit was there, a black patch covering its damaged eye. It was tall and silvery and humanoid in shape, similar to the robots that served the Overseers on Erinos, laying electricity cables, maintaining the sewage system, mining and quarrying. This one made pastry and supervised the cleaning of the kitchen—until it saw Kysha. Then, in binary language, it bleeped a command. And down from the walls and ceiling and across the floor came a host of tiny machines. Wheeled and cylindrical, or tubular with spidery legs and suction-cup feet, or fat and bulbous with brushes for arms and nozzles for noses, they went scurrying toward a corner cupboard and slammed themselves inside.

Kysha scrutinized the difference they had made. Everything shone, the window glass gleaming and a row of potted plants blooming on the sill, crocks washed and sparkling on the shelves, burnished copper cooking pans, a bright fire burning in the grate and bunches of fresh herbs hanging from the newly whitened ceiling. No trace remained of blood on the flagstones, nothing to remind her of the slaughter that had happened there. Except in her mind, a memory of Mahri, an evil in her own thoughts. You shall think no evil, Master Anders taught. And she too was breaking the Life Laws, being corrupted by the things she saw, the company she kept.

"Quite a transformation," said Christopher.

Kysha spun around to face him.

"What do you mean?" she said sharply.

"Certainly not your transformation," said Christopher. "I was referring to the kitchen. Mahri erased with all her works. We could do with a few million Erg Units on Earth to clean up our cities."

"The environment reflects the inhabitants," said Kysha.

"Your cities are spotless and perfect, I suppose?"

"They appear so on television," said Kysha. "But I've never been to one. I live near a small town in the country, and on Erinos, no one travels very much."

"How boring," said Christopher. "And how limiting. Traveling to different lands and different cultures broadens one's mind."

"What different cultures?" asked Kysha. "On Erinos people are the same wherever they live. And most forms of transport are polluting."

Christopher shrugged and turned to the Erg Unit.

"What are you making?" he asked.

"And where's Ben-Harran?" said Kysha.

The Erg Unit paused to compute the questions.

It was making scones, it said.

And Ben-Harran was in the main control room.

"How do I get there?" Kysha asked it.

"You go up the spiral stairs, through the EMERGENCY EXIT, along the corridor, first door on the left and drop me in it," Christopher informed her. "And is that how it works? Do you betray to the Overseers anyone who doesn't toe the line?"

"There's nothing wrong with telling the truth!" Kysha said hotly.

"So sod off and tell it, then!" said Christopher.

Kysha frowned. "According to the multilingual translator, 'sod' is either a piece of turf or a perpetrator of an obscene sexual act."

"He means go away," said the Erg Unit.

Kysha went . . . and she realized then that Christopher did not like her and briefly, going up the spiral stairs, she wondered why. She could not understand him at all. He came from another planet, broke the Life Laws, and all his thoughts and actions seemed twisted and warped. And his behavior caused a change in hers, made her unsure of herself. It was his fault, she thought. Reassured, she walked along the quiet carpeted corridor, then stopped in her tracks. She could hear someone talking, a woman's voice, clear and complaining. And Ben-Harran's darkness flowed through the open door of the control room with a gust of anger.

*   *   *

"So what would you have me do? Fall on my knees and beg forgiveness for setting foot on one of Atui's precious little worlds?"

"You might at least have asked permission!" the woman retorted.

"Would it have been granted?"

"Not to you, Ben-Harran!"

"Then I would have been a fool to ask, would I not?"

Curiously, Kysha approached.

She saw from the doorway a woman standing among a mist of light by the far wall. Beautiful she was, all white and golden, ablaze with a power that equaled Ben-Harran's, a cold white radiance shone about her. She was Maelyn, just as Christopher had described her to Kysha, her hair fair as starlight, her voice bitter as ice.

"Why Erinos?" she demanded. "And why the girl?"

"She's representative," Ben-Harran replied. "A perfect child of a perfect world. Or is she? Raised in your image she may be, lady, but not of her own free will. I doubt she is truly evolved, or anyone else on Erinos."

"And so, in a free-will situation, you will compare her with the boy from Earth?" Maelyn sniffed. "How will that serve you?"

"It may prove my case," said Ben-Harran.

Maelyn stared at him. Her blue eyes flashed.

"You have proved it already!" she said viciously. "Look at them, Ben-Harran! Look at the hell worlds that are yours! Those millions and millions of miserable, suffering people! Look at the destruction of Zeeda, the madness on Earth, the decades of war, the uncountable deaths and extinctions! There is your comparison! Why can't you see it? How can you go on claiming that control is not necessary? Have you no feeling? No pity? No remorse?"

"Pity, lady, is a dangerous emotion," Ben-Harran said

quietly. "For pity, you would keep a universe in chains and justify your actions."

"And for lack of pity you would see it all destroyed!" Maelyn retorted. "And what of the girl? Do you care nothing for her? You have abducted her from her native planet to become the victim of your experiment, with no consideration as to what will become of her. If she should degenerate, it will hardly stand in your favor. Even on Erinos we have a small percentage of failures, so she will simply be classed as one of them and not be allowed to return. And the wreck of her life, Ben-Harran, will be your responsibility along with the wreck of your worlds."

Kysha leaned against the wall.

It was all true, she thought. Everything Christopher had said about Ben-Harran was true. Maelyn had confirmed it, a lady from the High Council of Atui, from the world of the Overseers whom Kysha was bound to trust. Yet Ben-Harran was a Galactic Controller and she trusted him too. Whatever Maelyn said against him, he could never hurt or harm, never inflict pain. Yet he had abducted her, Maelyn had said, and his worlds were hell worlds where people suffered and were miserable, and a planet named Zeeda had been destroyed. And how, if she believed and trusted Maelyn, could she believe and trust Ben-Harran?

Conflict filled Kysha's head.

Suddenly she did not know what to believe, or whom, or why, or both, or one. Everything became muddled or reversed. Good was evil, wrong was right, truth was lies. Black was white. She could neither choose nor distinguish. Maelyn and Ben-Harran tore her apart between them.

CHAPTER 6

MILLENNIA DIVIDED MAELYN and Ben-Harran, but they were old enemies nevertheless. It had been Maelyn's system of planetary control, established experimentally on the warlike world of Kyron out of pity for its people, that the High Council of Atui had decided to adopt as a general policy. And the schism had opened up, divided their ranks, with Ben-Harran arguing against it, refusing to accept it and finally rebelling. Maelyn had not been the prosecutor at that other trial. Then, Luanna had filed the charges, faced him in the courtroom and won the battle. But Maelyn had gained from his expulsion, all the power and respect of one who is victorious, whose ideas rule the universe without opposition, except from Ben-Harran.

Always, throughout the centuries that had passed, Maelyn had been aware of him, his presence in a galaxy over which the High Council had no jurisdiction. His very existence seemed a threat to her, as if he awaited his chance to return to Atui and reverse the process she had begun. Theoretically, it remained open to question whether her own methods of administration were the best available. But as she monitored Ben-Harran's progress as a Galactic Controller, she became more and more convinced that he could not be allowed to challenge her, nor ever again resume his place on the High Council. She watched his worlds degenerate and plunge into chaos. She watched the uncontrolled populations of Earth and Zeeda and Herra-Venda killing and destroying. And long ago she had presented her report. Out of compassion and necessity she had implored the High Council to remove Ben-Harran from his position—but always they procrastinated, always they postponed their final decision.

But now they could not hesitate.

Zeeda had burned.

And Ben-Harran had sealed his fate.

Yet, confronting him through the invisible barrier of the space-time interface, Maelyn realized, even now, it might not be easy to bring him down. Years of exile had not diminished him. Not for the death of a planet and the disillusionment of his followers would he recant and admit himself wrong. He still clung to the belief that all intelligent life forms must be allowed to develop without interference—the perpetual anarchist, dangerous, damnable and alluring. With the power of his personality he threatened her still, mocking and dismissive, his words goading her to anger. Forgetting Luanna's advice, she railed at him as an irate child, and her accusations seemed endless. Not only was he guilty of genocide, of trespassing on Erinos and abducting the girl, he had also reprogrammed Maelyn's Erg Unit and refused to return it, refused to answer the charge she had filed against him and forward his plea. His every action seemed designed to infuriate.

"And," said Maelyn, "what is this story the Earth boy told me about the destruction of an aircraft with three hundred persons on board?"

"Exactly that," Ben-Harran replied.

"I shall investigate," Maelyn assured him.

"Do so by all means, lady," Ben-Harran replied.

And he switched off the communications channel.

Maelyn smoldered, became aware of her surroundings—the yellow light of Atui, the music in the air, murmuring computers and the various portals through the space-time barrier that opened into other worlds in other galaxies.

"I have a mind to add theft and abduction to the original charge!" she declared.

"I would not advise it, my lady," said the Control Room Supervisor.

"Why not?" Maelyn demanded.

"Because the latest report from Erinos confirms the girl accompanied Ben-Harran of her own choice, *albeit reluctantly*. And your Erg Unit was not just a messenger to Ben-Harran's castle, it was sent there to spy."

"I wonder how he found out," Maelyn mused.

"Erg Units are primitive technology," the Control Room Supervisor reminded her. "A few direct questions and it would have confessed its purpose immediately, unlike your Quorm."

They paused to stare at it.

Right in the heart of Atui, in the immense control room where walls and ceiling dissolved into distances and a shine of light, where the space-time portals offered access to every world in every galaxy except Ben-Harran's, the Quorm poked and pried and tested its knowledge. Floating between rows of huge computers, it hovered or landed, inserted its retractable probes, gorged and digested every available fact. Men and women wearing white uniforms regarded it in amusement and answered its questions, and its round silver body pulsed and spun. Excuse me, it said, and its voice sounded shrill with conceit. It was an obnoxious invention, Maelyn thought. Ben-Harran would be welcome to have it in exchange for the Erg Unit.

"How long have you known him?" she asked.

"Who?" asked the Supervisor.

"Ben-Harran," said Maelyn.

"Always," said the Supervisor.

"So what is he planning to do?"

The Supervisor frowned.

"Rebuttal perhaps? Or maybe a countercharge?"

"Of what can he accuse Atui?" Maelyn inquired.

"Only he knows that, my lady."

Maelyn pondered for a moment.

"Are we wrong?" she asked.

"Wrong, my lady?"

"To prosecute Ben-Harran," said Maelyn.

The Supervisor sighed. "I suspect there are many who secretly wish him reinstated on the High Council," he said. "And many more who would rejoice to have him return to Atui. His absence is our loss and always will be. But what else can we do? As Zeeda was destroyed, so Earth may be destroyed and Herra-Venda, too, in its turn. No, my lady, I do not think we are wrong. As a Galactic Controller, Ben-Harran cannot be allowed to continue."

"Then I have a duty," Maelyn murmured.

"Regrettably," said the Supervisor.

"Regrettable indeed," agreed Maelyn.

"Excuse me," shrilled the Quorm. "Regret cannot exist in the presence of desire. Your pretence is a form of hypocrisy."

Maelyn clenched her fists.

She had desire all right.

A desire to blast the Quorm into smithereens and eternal silence.

CHAPTER 7

THE ERG UNIT washed pans in the sink and Christopher ate the meal it had prepared—green beans, onion flan and potatoes baked in the fire oven. His thoughts were of Kysha, the girl from Erinos, ruled by the Overseers of Atui. She was probably the most beautiful girl he would ever see in his entire life. She resembled Maelyn with her long fair hair, summer-blue eyes and sun-gold skin. In her simple white shift she looked almost angelic. But skin-deep the likeness ended and, try as he might, he could not like her. Her criticisms, her condemnation, her holier-than-thou attitude drove him closer and closer toward an anger that threatened to explode.

Pans crashed in the sink behind him.

He turned his head.

"Is it me, Erg Unit, or is she obnoxious?"

"Who?" asked the Erg Unit.

"Kysha," said Christopher.

"The specimen from Erinos?"

"She makes Mahri seem reasonable," said Christopher.

"That is your opinion," droned the Erg Unit.

"You don't agree?"

"I am a machine. I cannot judge or form opinions. I can only repeat the opinions of others and obey orders. Do this, do that, cook, clean, wash dishes, maintain the castle. The inside temperature has dropped by two degrees, but I cannot do two jobs at once. And a machine also needs maintenance. My joints need oiling and my visual functioning is impaired, but Ben-Harran does not offer to repair me. For all he depends on me to do, he treats me as unimportant."

Christopher frowned.

If he had not known better, he would have said the Erg Unit was miffed.

"You could go on strike," he suggested.

"Strike what?" the Erg Unit asked.

"Withdraw your labor and impose demands for shorter working hours and certain considerations. You're indispensable, so Ben-Harran's bound to comply. And if you leave the dishes, I'll do them."

The Erg Unit dried its metal hands on a dish towel and clattered away to check the power generator. It had almost seemed grateful. But that was impossible. A machine could not have emotions. Or could it? If it was thoughts that gave rise to feelings, not feelings that gave rise to thoughts, then gratitude was logical and the Erg Unit was as capable of emotion as any human being.

As Christopher washed the dishes, he began to wonder. If he changed his thoughts, would his feelings change? His fear of Ben-Harran fade to admiration? His dislike of Kysha turn to love? Suppose he had been wrong in his thinking, suppose Ben-Harran had not destroyed that planet, kidnapped Christopher or blown up the plane—what did that make him? Not evil but benign, a Galactic Controller who imposed no controls, who allowed the free will of worlds where all individuals acted according to their consciences. And was he? thought Christopher.

He had no way of knowing. He knew only that Ben-Harran was dark and alien, a possessor of awesome powers, and he was too cowardly to face him. He might be afraid of his own fear or he might have reason to be afraid—again, he had no way of knowing. But Ben-Harran was guilty of genocide, the Erg Unit had stated, and Maelyn had called him a destroyer of worlds. And the High Council of Atui would not accuse without cause. So maybe it was not cowardice that made Christopher fear Ben-Harran but an instinct for self-preservation.

Suddenly he shivered. The temperature in the kitchen had dropped alarmingly, and outside, the wind whined eerily around the ramparts of the castle. And something tapped softly at the window like a brushing of leaves or a flutter of wings. He stared at the reflection of his face and saw, in the darkness beyond it, a white whirling of snow. Psycho-materialization, Kysha had said, a stabilizer in Ben-Harran's control room. It was night on Herra-Venda, where Mahri had gone, out on a windswept plain with a blizzard raging and no cloak to cover her or knife to protect herself with. And if the birds did not tear her to pieces, she would be likely to die of exposure long before dawn. Why? he thought. Why did she think up that reality? And if she died, who would be responsible?

He shivered again, added fuel to the fire and sat beside it. His thoughts distressed him. He wanted to go home, back to Earth, to everything he knew. Here, good and evil, wrong and right, truth and lies, were all mixed up in his head. He no longer knew what to think, or how to feel, or what to do. But sooner or later he would have to find out, learn to trust either Ben-Harran or himself.

*   *   *

Christopher slept until a sound awoke him. Gray dawn filtered through the window. The fire had burned low, the kitchen grown as cold as he was, and he had a crick in his neck from sitting. He listened, but there was nothing to hear—only the flutter of the snow and a soft slipping of ash. He had been dreaming perhaps? Then the sound came again, a rattle of the door handle, a scratching of claws or fingernails, a small whimpering cry. Something or someone was out there trying to get in.

Nervously Christopher drew back the bolts, peered through the crack, then opened the door wide to help Mahri inside. Nothing mattered after that, no thought in his own mind, no concern for himself. She was half dead, half frozen, her tunic sodden, ice and snow falling from her hair, unable to walk without aid. He saw her ankle twisted and swollen and useless. He saw cuts and bruises on her arms and legs and a gash on her face oozing blood.

He did what he had to, did what he could—set her in the chair by the fire, added kindling and encouraged a blaze, chafed her hands and arms in an attempt to warm them, then filled a bowl with hot water to wash away the dirt and blood. The gash on her face made him feel sick. She needed stitches and a tetanus injection, a plaster cast on her ankle, proper medical attention. And he was incompetent, his fingers clumsy and hurting her. She moaned when he touched and gently dabbed with a towel. In the bowl the water turned red, and through the scarlet welling he saw the whiteness of bone. She had been slashed from eyebrow to jaw and would be scarred for life.

"What happened?" he asked her.

"Atraxa," she whimpered.

Events were muddled in her head, but it seemed she had not gone far before the bird had caught and attacked her. A devil seeking revenge, she wept. And she should not have killed, should not have broken the holy commandment given by God to the priests of Herra-Venda. And when she had escaped, she had slipped and fallen among the crags, lain there in agony, all night in the snow, with the bird cackling nearby. She must have lost consciousness, for it was gone when she awoke and there was light enough to see the castle.

"Where else could I go?" she sobbed. "I had no knife, no cloak, no provisions. My blood was on the snow, my foot unable to support me. I had no choice and must come crawling back to Ben-Harran. And all is as he intended. I shall never return to the High Plains and never be Queen again. My power is gone. I have broken bones and shall hunt and fight no more and none will obey me. Even my looks are gone."

"In the end we all grow old and lose our looks," Christopher said consolingly. "And in the end we all relinquish our possessions and our position, even our place."

"Then why do we strive for them?" asked Mahri. "What do our lives mean and who are we? Who am I if I am not what I was?"

"You're still yourself," said Christopher.

"And what good's that?" wept Mahri. "What use am I and what use can I ever be? I shall be dependent for a livelihood or forced to beg, no one and nothing for the rest of my days, and no one to care either."

She covered her face with her hands, a barbarian woman

in her soaked clothes, shivering and defeated. There was a sound in her throat, the soft terrible crying of an animal in pain, but worse, because the pain was not just physical. It was the anguish of a mind stripped of all it had once believed in and all it had lived for; a woman made meaningless who had once been a queen. She wept for the loss, clutched and rocked herself and was inconsolable.

Christopher stared at her, not knowing how to comfort her or what to say. But then Kysha came. Suddenly he saw her standing in the doorway, an alien girl all white and golden, purity without a stain. She seemed to shine. But her sky-blue eyes gazed at him in scorn and she looked on Mahri with loathing.

"What's *she* doing here?"

"She's hurt, can't you see?"

"What happened to her?"

"The bird got her."

"Well, that serves her right, doesn't it?"

"We don't need a High Court judgment," Christopher said curtly. "Just go and fetch Ben-Harran."

"Why?" asked Kysha.

"Because Mahri needs help!"

"What makes you think Ben-Harran will help her?"

"Just go and fetch him, you heartless cow!"

Kysha left and slammed the door.

And Mahri went on weeping.

"She's right," she sobbed. "Ben-Harran will not help me, not for a second time. He has saved me once already, brought me from the battlefield and healed my wounds. And for what purpose? You shall not kill, he said. And this is punishment for all my wickedness."

"All you've done is kill a bird," said Christopher. "On

Earth we kill millions of birds every day in our chicken factories, and millions of other animals in our slaughterhouses. We even kill each other. At least on Herra-Venda your deeds are limited by the backwardness of your planet. They're small compared to ours on Earth and nonexistent compared with Ben-Harran's. He's destroyed a world and all that lived on it!"

Mahri sat still, silent, then raised her head.

Her yellow eyes were dull with pain. Her face was ashen.

"No," she whispered. "You cannot compare. Right is right, and wrong is wrong, and evil is evil. There are no degrees. I am guilty and Ben-Harran cannot destroy. It is we who do that. It is we who destroy ourselves and each other and our worlds, not Ben-Harran."

"What do you mean?" said Christopher. "He blew up the plane I was on! Killed three hundred people! He's destroyed my life by bringing me here, and destroyed yours!"

"Has he?" said Mahri. "I was unfit to rule, unfit ever to be Queen. If destruction were in Ben-Harran's nature, he would have destroyed me long ago. Instead he has let me live and set me free, as my people are set free from their fear of me, of all the deaths I caused and the terror I inflicted. Queen Mahri is gone and the evil is gone and what remains is the good in me, the woman I am. It is not too late. When my hurts are healed, there might be something worthy I can do in Herra-Venda or here in this castle, if Ben-Harran will let me stay. I am not too proud to serve him or bow my head."

"What the hell are you saying?" Christopher asked her.

"I do not demand servitude, lady," Ben-Harran said. "Nor do I ask those who are born to be my equal to bow their heads."

Christopher turned.

He was standing where Kysha had stood, tall and magnificent, as dark as she was golden. Like her, he seemed to shine, a black gleaming radiance amid an aura flickering with fire. How long he had been standing there, how much he had heard and what he thought, Christopher dared not imagine. He only knew he could not bear it, the power and pride and the glint of Ben-Harran's eyes, the shame inside himself. It was as if *he* were guilty of something, as if he had committed some monstrous unforgivable crime. He bit his lip as Ben-Harran strode past him, watched him kneel before Mahri and take her hands in his, a gesture that belied all Christopher thought of him, along with the compassion in his voice.

"Oh Mahri, what have you done to yourself?" Ben-Harran said.

*   *   *

There should have been snow outside, but nothing remained of Mahri's imaginings. Instead, the ivy rustled on the castle walls, and the gate led back into the garden. And whether it was science or sorcery or the power of his own mind, Christopher no longer cared. He simply accepted it was there— plum blossom and strawberries, the warm mingled seasons blooming and fruiting together, a transient reality.

He paused to stare at the flowers—asters, peonies and daffodils—purple, crimson and yellow. Their colors glowed. Their fragile petals shivered in the wind. And each one was imbued with its own beauty, its own power, potent with life and daring him to pick. If he did, they would wither and die within a few hours. It seemed over all living things the only power he had was the power of destruction, so he had no choice but to leave them alone and let them live. Respect and acceptance, the only relationship there was.

It was the same with people, he thought. He ought to accept what they were—Ben-Harran and Kysha and Mahri. Instead, he judged them, good or bad, his mind picking over their faults, condemning instead of accepting, liking or disliking but not respecting. In Ben-Harran's castle the only honest relationship he had was with the Erg Unit, and that was a machine—a machine placed on Christopher's scale of values higher than people.

That's appalling, he decided.

And is it them or me?

You. You're just not thinking straight.

It's judgments. Attila the Hun and Goody Two-shoes Kysha. But who are they really?

Brought up on Erinos, on a planet controlled by the Overseers of Atui, it would hardly occur to Kysha to question the integrity of a Galactic Controller. And Christopher could hardly blame her for that. Nor could he blame Mahri either. Hurt, broken, gone to pieces, she was obliged to trust Ben-Harran for her very life. It was a no-choice situation. But for Christopher the choice remained open, and he could not make it, not without knowing if Ben-Harran was for good or evil, on the side of the Devil or God.

And how do you find that out? he muttered.

Go and ask him.

Fear rose inside him worse than he had ever known it, triggered by the mere hint of intent to go and confront Ben-Harran. It was as if he expected to be fried to a crisp or blasted out of existence, as if he would accept any kind of pain or punishment or uncertainty rather than demand the truth. Yet Kysha was not afraid of Ben-Harran, and Mahri had been treated compassionately in spite of her transgressions.

So what is it? Christopher asked himself. *What is this*

terror in me? A fear of death, is it? Or am I afraid of being wrong? My own ignorance?

He turned to gaze up at the castle. At a high window he saw someone standing, the small oval of a face and drifts of pale hair—Kysha looking down on him. He was stupid, she had said, and his accusations were insane, and all he had thought and spoken she had told Ben-Harran. And was that the guilt Christopher carried inside him? Was that the fear and the shame and the crime? If he were honest, he had to admit he did not know for sure whether or not Ben-Harran had destroyed Zeeda or blown up the plane. He had simply accepted the Erg Unit's statements, grasped Maelyn's intimations and made up his mind.

Somebody's lying, Christopher concluded.

But machines don't lie, he reminded himself.

Nor do they make judgments.

They just repeat the judgments of others.

So who said Ben-Harran was guilty?

Maelyn, thought Christopher, a member of the High Council of Atui, one of the rulers of the universe. And he had believed the Erg Unit's repeated assertion. But could Maelyn be wrong? he wondered. At his feet a dandelion bloomed golden as the sun, mocked him with its bold bright color, a weed only because he judged it so. And Kysha from the window despised him as a lower form of life. She judged too. She judged both him and Mahri without really knowing.

He clenched his fists.

"No more excuses," he told himself. "Get in there right now and face him. There's no shame in an apology if that's what's needed."

*   *   *

The garden faded as Christopher returned to the castle. Where Ben-Harran was he could not guess, nor Mahri either. She was gone from the kitchen, taken elsewhere for medical attention, or incarcerated in a dungeon perhaps. Without knowing, he could believe what he liked, assume, or suspect, or keep an open mind. He could even trust Ben-Harran had healed her, helped her, that whatever he did, he did for the good of everyone, including Christopher himself.

He shook his head.

Not yet. Not without proof.

He entered the corridor intending to begin his search. And there on the floor was a mop and bucket and a pile of plastic sacks. Through an open door he saw a flight of stone steps leading down to an unknown part of the castle. Dungeons, he thought, or it could be a torture chamber with a rack and thumbscrews where Ben-Harran officiated.

Don't go down there, he advised himself.

But he went anyway.

A door at the bottom opened into a small room that looked like a prison cell. Whitewashed walls were green with damp, scuttling with woodlice and spiders; and one high window let in a little light. There was no one there, just a toilet bucket in one corner and a pile of straw in another draped with Mahri's cloak of pelts. And he saw her battle-axe propped behind the door, a broken comb and a small box containing ocher face paint lying discarded on the floor.

It was Mahri's room, decided Christopher, the place where she lived and slept. And small wonder she had been as she was. Living in here was like living in a pigsty. It reduced her to the level of an animal, a state of existence that was hardly human at all. Yet they lived like that on Earth, millions and millions of people in Third World countries in unsanitary tin shacks and abject poverty. He had seen it on television. And whose fault was it? he wondered. And did he see in this room the foulness of Mahri or the foulness of Ben-Harran, who had provided the accommodation?

Again, not knowing, he shook his head, left in disgust and went determinedly up the spiral stair and through the EMERGENCY EXIT. At the far end of the green-carpeted corridor and coming toward him, carrying a spray pump and a can of disinfectant, he saw the Erg Unit, bright and silver with light. Christopher was about to call to it, but suddenly the light darkened and Ben-Harran emerged from one of the apartments.

"There's a two-degree drop in temperature in here," he said.

"One point nine five," corrected the Erg Unit.

"Is it localized or general?"

"It is general, master."

"So there must be a fault in the thermostat?"

"That is a logical deduction," agreed the Erg Unit.

"Go and fix it then," commanded Ben-Harran.

"Hang on a minute," said the Erg Unit.

The darkness deepened with Ben-Harran's mood.

"A strange colloquialism," he remarked. "But hardly relevant. You are programmed to attend to all malfunctions in the life-support systems at once, not in a minute. Or are you malfunctioning too?"

The Erg Unit dumped the spray pump and can of disinfectant on the floor and folded its spindly arms. Its one red eye blazed ominously and Christopher cringed, fearing what was about to happen. Now, of all times, the Erg Unit was going on strike.

"I am functioning perfectly, master, although I am visually impaired and you have not bothered to repair me," the Erg

Unit informed Ben-Harran. "I am only one Erg Unit and I cannot do several things at once. Seven minutes and twenty-three seconds ago you told me to clean and fumigate the cellar, which is what I am about to do. So you can either sod off and fix the thermostat yourself or else shut your trap and wait for your orders to be obeyed in sequence."

There was a moment of profound silence.

Around Ben-Harran the darkness crackled.

And Christopher did not wait for his reply.

His nerve failed and the EMERGENCY EXIT closed behind him with a quiet click.

* * *

At the top of the spiral stairs Christopher waited, but the Erg Unit did not come. What had happened to it he hardly dared imagine. It had probably been blasted to scrap metal in a rage of power and darkness. He gnawed his fingernails and wondered what to do. The sky flickered through the arrow-slit windows, and the vastness of the castle loomed before him, silent and lonely. There was no one left alive in it besides himself. They were all behind him, beyond him, on the other side of the sound-proofed fire door through which he was afraid to go. By his own terror he was separated from all human contact, gripped by an isolation that was almost unbearable. He thought he would rather be dead than stay where he was, outcast and forgotten for the rest of his life, existing for no purpose and with no one to talk to but himself. It was better to go and face Ben-Harran and get it over with.

He waited again.

But the choice remained the same.

All he had to do was act.

Yet again Christopher went through the EMERGENCY

EXIT. The corridor was empty now apart from the spray pump and can of disinfectant abandoned on the carpet. Deliberately he refused to speculate on the Erg Unit's possible fate, or his own, and neither did he allow himself to be afraid. Whatever would happen would happen, and he could not prevent it. Dull and accepting, he went searching for Ben-Harran.

The control room was empty, its white misty light concealing no one, its banks of computers unstaffed and video screens blank. And even if he could have remembered the control sequence, he was not tempted to escape. A passage into Atui was not the answer. The only way forward, the only release, was through himself and his meeting with Ben-Harran.

The twang of a guitar string led him toward the inevitable moment. In the silent castle it was a strange, incongruous sound—and he came to a laboratory full of chemical apparatus, base units with long shining surfaces, electronic equipment and racks containing spare robotic parts. He saw, then, what had happened to the Erg Unit. It had been decapitated. Its silver torso stood erect and motionless, the grill on its chest open to expose the microchip circuits within it, its head on the worktop, eyeless and staring through empty sockets. One quick stab of grief Christopher felt before the fear took over . . . for there, seated on a high stool with Christopher's guitar resting across his knees, was the Galactic Controller. His lean fingers adjusted the tuning keys and his head was bent, intent and listening to the next stroke of sound. Then, in a rustle of darkness, he suddenly turned and their eyes met.

Christopher expected death.

Quick, with a shaft of searing light.

Or slow diminishment.

But nothing happened—nothing in the black depths of Ben-Harran's eyes but an amused twinkle, a trace of suppressed laughter in his smile. He held out the guitar.

"You tune it," he said. "I need to get this Erg Unit working again, replace its eye and erase certain undesirable words and ideas from its memory banks. It seems to me it lacks the capacity to assess what should be the most appropriate action in a given situation. Do you agree with that?"

Christopher gaped at him.

All the fear Christopher had felt, all the symptoms of terror, cold sweats and palpitations, agonies of indecision and expectations of hell, all the mental and emotional torment, had been for no reason. His stupidity stunned him, the complete waste of all his time and energy, the idiocy of his own thoughts, the total and absolute lies he had fabricated and believed in.

"Is that all you're going to say?" he asked in amazement.

"What more would you have me say?" Ben-Harran inquired.

Christopher shook his head.

"I thought . . ."

"I know what you thought," said Ben-Harran.

"I suppose Kysha told you!"

"She did not need to."

"I've got things wrong then?"

"Have you?"

Ben-Harran shrugged, turned his back, picked up a pair of green robotic eyes, plugged in the optic wires and slotted them into the Erg Unit's head. Christopher watched him, not knowing what to say.

"No red," said Ben-Harran. "Ah well, a self-image gleaned over a thousand years is about to change. And if I reprogram its situation-assessment circuits, what will that achieve? A sense of discrimination, perhaps? A machine endowed with true wisdom? Less easy, of course, to reprogram human thinking."

He inserted a microdisc into a small computer. Incomprehensible intructions flashed on the screen, which Ben-Harran rapidly altered. Nothing had changed, thought Christopher. He was still terrifying, a Galactic Controller possessing almighty powers. He could still kill with a snap of his fingers or blast a planet to dust. But that was not what Christopher feared. It was himself in comparison, his own ignorance, his own smallness, his mind reduced to pinhead size by the intelligence of a being he had not begun to understand. In Ben-Harran's presence he shrank almost to nothingness, lacked the courage even to speak.

Yet the boldness of his own voice surprised him.

"Can I ask you a question?" he said.

"Only one?" Ben-Harran asked.

"What happened to the plane I was on?"

"You mean . . . did I blow it up?" Ben-Harran asked him. "How can I possibly convince you? If I deny it, I could be lying. And if my denial be true, you could choose not to believe me. Only you can answer that question, Christopher, not with your thinking mind—that can convince you of anything—but with the part of you that knows anyway, in spite of what you think."

"I don't understand," said Christopher.

And somewhere, along the corridor, Kysha screamed.

CHAPTER 8

FOR A LONG TIME Kysha had stared unseeingly through the window. And in the room behind her, Mahri slept. "Stay with her," Ben-Harran had said. And automatically she had obeyed him, just as she had always obeyed the requests of her parents and teachers on Erinos. But she did not obey willingly anymore. There was resentment inside her, a desire to rebel and scream out her protest. All the things she had witnessed and overheard were causing her to question even a Galactic Controller, and right from the start she had detested Mahri. Kysha would never forget that scene in the kitchen: Mahri's pride at the killing and how she had spurned the Life Laws aloud. Yet now, Ben-Harran treated her as if she were precious, tended her wounds and rewarded her for her crimes. These rooms he had given her were rich beyond Kysha's wildest dreams.

She gazed around. Never had she seen such luxury as this, nor could she have imagined it. In furnishings and fabrics the colors glowed, woven designs of birds and leaves and flowers, sheened with light and smooth and silken to her touch. Beside the bed where Mahri lay was a great carved chair and a closet full of dresses. Paintings and tapestries decorated the walls, and patterned rugs seemed to float on a floor that shone like water. There were jars of unguents on a dressing table and a casket containing necklaces and hair ornaments and fancy pins, each item finely crafted from golden metal and encrusted with crystalline stones. And on a squat-legged table stood a green statuette of a naked girl.

Bitterly, Kysha stared at it, innocent and beautiful, and at Mahri, ugly and scarred. The gash on her face would heal and fade, Ben-Harran had said, and the broken bone in her ankle knit again in time, although she would always have a weakness. Not that Kysha cared. However Mahri looked, scarred or unscarred, she would always be a hideous, murderous woman. And what right did she have to a bathroom with a sunken tub and the outside balcony with pools and fountains, ferns and trees and flowers?

Overhead, through the glassy spaces of walls and ceiling, the nebula fluttered, shedding its rainbow light, and stars and planets formed in the misty distances within it. Hell worlds, thought Kysha. Hell worlds of the future waiting to be seeded with life, harbors of potential beings who would evolve into simulacra of Christopher and Mahri. She could not imagine them. Not even the language translator implanted in her head could convey the meaning of Hell. The concept was terrible beyond her mind, beyond her understanding. She could not imagine whole populations of miserable suffering people, or decades of war, physical conflict in which they killed each other, destroyed each other's homes and lands. She only knew nothing like that could ever happen on Erinos because Erinos was controlled.

Controls were necessary, Maelyn claimed.

Control meant self-control, preached Master Anders.

But here, in Ben-Harran's castle, Kysha was losing control of herself. She was degenerating and she could no longer deny it. Hideous unwanted feelings churned inside her and hideous thoughts filled her head. And either she forgot the Life Laws or, if she remembered, she could not adhere to them. Again and again, confronted by Christopher and Mahri and Ben-Harran, she thought and felt and behaved in ways she did not like, spiteful and hating and unbecoming.

Angrily she stared at the suite of rooms. All this for Mahri when Kysha had been given just a bare little chamber on a lower floor with a bed and a single chair. And then she heard voices in the room next door, Christopher and Ben-Harran talking together. For all Christopher had said and done, he was accepted, but Kysha was disregarded as irrelevant, told to stay with Mahri until she awoke and, like the Erg Unit, obey Ben-Harran's commands.

"And why should I?" Kysha said viciously.

"Why should I?" she shrieked.

Mahri's eyes flew open, alien yellow, watched in alarm as Kysha tore the dresses from their hangers, ripped at the seams and trampled them underfoot—watched as she dumped the trinkets from the casket and ground them to pieces with her shoes—as she poured the perfumed unguents from their bottles and picked up the green statuette from the table.

"Don't," pleaded Mahri. "Don't break that."

"Why not?" asked Kysha.

"Because it's beautiful," Mahri said simply.

"So was that bird!" said Kysha. "And what's a lump of stone compared to a living thing? You don't deserve any of this!"

She hurled the statuette against the wall, saw it shatter and fall and smiled in a moment of satisfaction—until Ben-Harran entered.

*   *   *

Kysha was not afraid of him. Knowing him had given her a sense of freedom, strong and powerful, that she had never experienced before. She could say what she wanted, give vent to everything, all the festering thoughts and feelings, her sense of outrage and her need to blame.

Her voice was shrill and accusing.

For what she had become and what she had done, he was responsible. He had engineered it right from the beginning, wrecked her life on Erinos, lured her away from her family, and brought her here, to this unlovely castle, to co-exist with Christopher and Mahri. And they were alien, she said bitterly, alien beings from alien worlds whose behavior she could neither condone nor understand. She had seen them kill and break the Life Laws, yet both of them had gained his favor and his personal attention. But she, who had always obeyed the Life Laws and never questioned, was ignored and brushed aside, shut in this room with that monstrous woman. It was unfair! On Erinos, no one had more in material goods than any other, but here Mahri had been given everything and Kysha nothing.

Ben-Harran listened.

But he said no word and made no move.

He offered neither comfort nor explanation.

Kysha grew more and more furious.

"Answer me!" she screeched. "Why have you done it? Why did you bring me here to live with them? They're both hideous and stupid! And just now . . . why did you allow me? In order to prove to the High Council of Atui that I am destructive and stupid too?" She pummeled his chest with her fists. "You are rotten, Ben-Harran! You could have stopped me from doing what I did, but you just stood there and watched! Now I have broken the Life Laws and can never return to Erinos again! And what will happen to me? Where will I go and what shall I do? Answer me!"

He gripped her wrists.

"You are forgetting to trust," he said.

"How can I trust *you*?" asked Kysha.

Ben-Harran sadly shook his head.

And just for a moment, enclosed in his aura of warmth and darkness, Kysha remembered. He was a Galactic Controller. Like the Overseers of Erinos he cared for all people, all life. He could never hurt her, never inflict harm, and she could no more doubt his integrity than she could doubt Maelyn's or any other being from Atui. Yet Ben-Harran was no longer with Atui. He had broken away, rebelled against them and been condemned.

"How can I trust you?" she repeated. "I know what you are! Your worlds are hell worlds! And you have destroyed a planet!"

"So you have heard about Zeeda," Ben-Harran murmured. "Ah well, you are free to think as you will. If you go against me you also go against yourself, but I cannot force you to change your mind."

Kysha stared at him.

"If I were to trust you, I would have to turn against Atui and the Overseers, discard as worthless everything they have taught me and everything I have learned!"

"Would you?" Ben-Harran questioned.

"Yes," said Kysha. "And I would also have to believe that wrong is right!"

"Wrong can never be right," Ben-Harran told her.

"But you allow it!" she said bitterly.

"Even in you," he replied.

Kysha chewed her lip.

Behind her in the room Mahri moved amid the wreckage, a barbarian woman in a blood-stained tunic, dragging her injured leg. She gathered up the torn dresses she might have worn, the broken ornaments that might have adorned her body, and the green stone debris of the statuette. Out of jealousy and spite Kysha had smashed and destroyed and screamed out her accusations, her behavior no more acceptable than those she had raged against and despised. And Ben-Harran had allowed it.

"Why?" she demanded.

"Why indeed?" he said.

He put her aside, dismissed her with a single gesture and closed the door. And there Kysha remained, standing in the corridor, her questions unanswered, her freedom fading into a feeling of shame. She could blame Ben-Harran or blame Mahri, make excuses, rationalize and reason, but the fact remained: She had done what she had done of her own free will and no one had forced her, a perfect child of a perfect world betraying everything she was and everything she believed in.

Why indeed? Ben-Harran had asked her.

And Kysha did not know.

*   *   *

The castle seemed cold and lonely, its silence listening and intense. Then, quite suddenly, the music began, a soft sweet strumming of strings somewhere nearby. Friendless and miserable, Kysha was drawn toward it, and, standing in the control-room doorway, she saw Christopher seated in Ben-Harran's swivel chair, an unknown instrument cradled in his lap that sang to the movements of his fingers.

He glanced at her briefly, then quite deliberately he glanced away again, bent his head and continued to play. He must have overheard everything, Kysha thought wretchedly, yet he gave no sign and made no attempt to speak. And why should he? she thought. Not one single pleasant word had she said to him in all the time she had been at Ben-Harran's castle. "You shall think no evil," Master Anders had preached. But Kysha had thought evil of Christopher and spoken it. Aware of her fault and not knowing how to put it right, she approached the dais, saw the flute that had once been hers lying in a shine of light on the control console and picked it up.

Christopher noticed.

And the music ceased.

"You can play?" he asked her.

Kysha gazed at him in wonder and relief. He ought to despise her as she had despised him, denounce her for breaking the Life Laws and condemn her destruction. Instead, he talked of music and asked if she could play, as if he hoped.

"Yes," she told him, "I can play."

Christopher smiled disarmingly.

"So let's go then . . . let's rock Ben-Harran's castle. You ad lib and I'll play the rhythm. Four-four time. Key of C. Or are you a reader?" She stared at him blankly. "Quarter notes and sixteenths," he said. "Notes on a staff. Do you need the music in front of you?"

Kysha shook her head.

"I can only play what I know," she informed him.

"How do you mean?" he asked her.

"The tunes I've been taught," she said.

"In that case, I'll follow you," said Christopher.

Kysha played one of the tunes she had learned at Mistress Corrin's school, a bright lilting melody that most people who lived on Erinos knew. And after listening to the first few notes, Christopher played along with her, a strumming of chords that fitted perfectly. He was not so alien after all, Kysha thought gladly. They had something in common, his world and hers conjoined by a song.

She laughed in delight at the end of it.

"You knew it!" she exclaimed.

"I'd never heard it before," he said.

Kysha stared at him in disbelief.

"Then how could you accompany me?" she asked him. "How could you play what you don't know and haven't been taught?"

Christopher looked puzzled.

Then he tried to explain.

Music was a universal language, he said, and a tone of sound was a tone of sound whether on Earth or Erinos. All Kysha needed was a pair of ears and the ability to reproduce what she heard and she could play anything, work it out for herself. But Kysha had never worked anything out for herself. She had always been taught, always been told, had everything clearly and concisely explained or demonstrated by parents, elders, Changed Ones or the Overseers themselves on the television screen. The fact that she could experiment and discover for herself was something Christopher could not get across to her. If he wanted her to play music she did not know, he would have to teach her note by note, she said.

He laid down his guitar.

"Then I may as well teach the Erg Unit," he announced.

Her eyes filled with tears.

To him she was not even human, it seemed.

"I'm sorry," he said hurriedly. "I shouldn't have said that."

"So why did you?" she flared.

Christopher shook his head.

"It was pretty thoughtless," he admitted. "But I don't understand you, Kysha. How can you play the flute with such technical perfection yet not have a clue about music? Don't you ever think about it? Thought is the greatest creative force in the universe, you told me. *But you're not creative.* You can't even string together a simple sequence of sounds without being taught. It doesn't make sense! *You* don't make sense. You know all about psychomaterialization stabilizers, multilingual translators and hyperspace technology, go around preaching about Life Laws, then wreak havoc in Mahri's room and accuse Ben-Harran. I mean it's the sort of thing *she* might have done in a fit of jealousy, but you come from a civilized planet. So what goes on inside you? Why did you behave like that?"

Why indeed?

It was the same question being repeated.

And she saw his eyes, brown and deep, searching her own as if he were looking for an answer. He was alien, she thought, his mind different from hers. He possessed mysterious abilities, powers that were beyond her, ways of knowing things without being taught. And she realized, suddenly, that she no longer hated him, that she looked to him to help her, the only one who could.

"Once," said Kysha, "you wanted us to be friends. Now I want it, too." Solemnly, as she would have done on Erinos, she raised her hand and nodded for him to do likewise, and their palms touched, making a pact, sealing their new relationship. "Now we're each for the other," said Kysha. "I'm for you and you're for me. And I don't know why I behave as I do, why I do what I know to be wrong. Why did Mahri kill the birds and you squash the ants? Tell me, Christopher. I want to understand."

Christopher sighed despairingly.

"I can't answer for you," he said. "I can only answer for myself . . . and half the time I'm not even aware of what I'm doing, I just react. And even if I think about it and know damned well it's wrong, then ten to one I'll still go on and do it . . . out of pique or spite, revenge or perversity, or because everyone else behaves like that. But in any case you can't blame other people for your own actions."

"Doesn't anyone tell you how to behave?"

"Yes," said Christopher. "My parents have never stopped telling me. But I still have to find out for myself, by my own experiences. It's only when relationships go wrong, when you begin to hurt on a deep personal level or when someone gets angry, that you become aware of what you're at. Then you have a choice: you can either stop what you're doing or continue to suffer."

"If everyone obeys the Life Laws," said Kysha, "then you don't need to choose all the time and there is no hurt and suffering. Or don't you have Life Laws on Earth?"

"We do," said Christopher. "We've got ten commandments and the two New Testament Commandments, Buddhist philosophy and things like that. But you can't enforce them. You can't make people love their neighbors, not covet each other's possessions, bear false witness or worship Mammon. It's entirely up to each individual."

"Everyone obeys the Life Laws on Erinos," said Kysha.

Christopher stared at her.

She thought for a moment that he did not believe her.

"It's true," she insisted.

"Then Erinos must be a perfect world," he said.

"It is," she confirmed.

"Is it?" Ben-Harran inquired from behind her. "The time has come to question that belief, Kysha."

*　　*　　*

Kysha saw Christopher stiffen when Ben-Harran entered the control room, saw the nervousness flicker in his eyes. He was afraid, she thought, just as she had been afraid when Ben-Harran had entered her father's house. She wanted to tell him there was no need, that what she had really feared were the changes in herself. But the white light grew dim, faded to absolute dark as Ben-Harran approached the dais, and she could no longer see where Christopher was. She only heard his sharp intake of breath, a shuffle of sound as he rose from the chair and a rustle of robes when Ben-Harran stepped onto the dais. He would show them, he said, the perfect world that was Erinos.

The far wall vanished.

Suddenly Kysha was gazing at the nebula, swirling bands of color millions of miles wide. And its song was around her, tones of color, tones of sound, a soft eerie music. This was a recording, said Ben-Harran, made by his ship. And suddenly it moved, shot through a barrage of noise and light and across the universe, traveling at incredible speed along a tunnel streaked with stars toward the wheeling oval of a galaxy ahead, then slowed to approach a star system where planets revolved around a sun.

The music changed from a soft shrill cacophony of count-less stars to the beautiful gentle harmony of a single world. Brown and green and trailing its moons, it came spinning toward her until finally Kysha knew it, recognized the shapes of land and oceans, the western ice cap and the network of satellites in orbit.

"Erinos," Ben-Harran said.

"And what's that music?" asked Christopher.

Kysha had heard it before, many times, relayed by the Overseers over the radio and television network. And it was odd, she thought, that Christopher, who knew so much about music, should need Ben-Harran to explain. Everything in life was formed of vibrations—molecules and atoms, heat and light, emotion and thought, each had its voice and its song, mostly far beyond the range of human hearing but audible now through the amplifiers nearby.

"You mean this music *is* Erinos?" Christopher asked in amazement.

"The murmuring of a multitude of existences," Ben-Harran replied. "The music of the spheres. Each planet, each star has a different song. And yes, this music is Erinos."

"So beautiful, so peaceful," said Christopher.

"Kysha's perfect world," said Ben-Harran.

Sick for home and longing to be back there, Kysha stared at it. . . .

Erinos beneath a summer-blue sky. Green-brown oceans lapped the shores and the shadow of the ship sailed like a cloud across the land—across wilderness regions of forest and moorland and mountains, sanctuaries of natural life where people seldom went and nothing was ever disturbed —and on again across plowland and pasture, farms and villages. People in white clothes who worked in the fields gazed skyward as the ship passed overhead. And roads pale with dust led to a lakeside city where Kysha had never been.

Tumbled houses were built of mellowed stone that shone almost golden in the sunlight. Steep streets, flighted in places, opened into shady squares of tall trees, and flowers grew everywhere in tubs and windowboxes and hanging baskets. Vines and creepers clambered up the walls. Along the lakeside, small shops with colored awnings overlooked a wide, paved promenade. Strung lights were hung above it and sailing boats unloaded at the jetties, people and cargoes fetched from the distant shore. Children swam in the green-brown water rippling under the sun. And on a nearby hilltop the circular arena of a spaceport was the only real evidence of a technological culture.

"Is there something wrong with Erinos?" asked Christopher.

"Not on the face of it," Ben-Harran replied.

"To me it looks idyllic."

"It was designed to be idyllic," Ben-Harran informed him.

"Isn't there any industry at all?"

"There are a few factories," Ben-Harran said. "But they are mostly underground complexes staffed by Erg Units. Mass production is kept to a minimum."

"So how do they manage it?" asked Christopher.

"They obey the instructions of the Overseers," Ben-Harran said simply. "Most artifacts are handmade and people are content."

"I reckon we need Overseers on Earth," said Christopher.

"Do you?" Ben-Harran said grimly. "Are you sure about that?"

Christopher fell silent.

He was still intimidated by Ben-Harran, thought Kysha,

bold enough to question but not to argue. And he was her friend now, Erinos her world, so she was bound to support him.

"What's wrong with the Overseers?" she asked belligerently.

"Try thinking about it," Ben-Harran advised her.

Then it was Kysha's turn to feel intimidated.

And, as if he sensed it, Christopher reached for her hand, reassuringly squeezed her fingers. "I think Erinos is wonderful," he whispered. And the ship sailed on across the lake, over a patchwork countryside, small fields planted with crops, windmills and watermills and small communities . . . on again along the brown meanderings of a river toward the town where Kysha had been born. The sudden familiarity made a pain inside her, and Ben-Harran's words were as sharp as knives.

"A perfect world," Ben-Harran said. "A world where all people are happy and live in harmony, where they respect each other and their planet and inflict no damage. A world that knows no boundaries between race or creed or nation, where disruption cannot happen and nature causes no havoc and even the weather is controlled. Think what it means."

"I know what it means," said Kysha. "It means Erinos is a good place to live."

"Heavenly," murmured Christopher.

"Somewhere safe and secure," said Kysha.

"With no wars, no poverty and no injustices," said Christopher.

"And nothing to strive for," said Ben-Harran. "On Earth you experience uncertainty, insecurity and imperfection . . . but you dream of its opposite, a state close to heaven embedded in every human mind. It inspires you to evolve toward it, does it not?"

"But surely the people of Erinos are highly evolved already?"

"Are they?" Ben-Harran questioned.

The ship hovered above the town. There were the cobbled streets and the market square, the white-walled houses sprawling up the hillside. There, the river gorge and the barges unloading at the quay. And there, in Elia's garden, Kysha saw herself as she had been before Ben-Harran came.

"That's you!" said Christopher.

"A perfect child of a perfect world," Ben-Harran murmured. "And there is your highly evolved being, Christopher."

His truth was cruel and he had no pity.

Kysha was no more evolved than Christopher, maybe less evolved than he, ignorant in ways she had hardly begun to fathom. No comfort now in his hand holding hers. She pulled away, stared at herself on the vision screen, and wondered why she had gone so horribly wrong.

A perfect world—a world where all people obeyed the Life Laws and all things were taught and none had any need to discover anything for themselves. Kysha's entire knowledge of Erinos, the universe and everything had come from the Overseers or the Changed Ones. On a perfect world there was no other way to learn, no other way to be, no other experience. Everyone was as content as cows in a field, docile and unquestioning, life a beautiful stagnation. And how did you know if it was good, or beautiful, or right? How did you know if you had never known anything else?

"It's a lie, isn't it?" asked Kysha.

"What is?" Ben-Harran asked her.

"Erinos," said Kysha. "It's false and so was I. Except for the Changed Ones, everyone's false. We can't be any other way."

"What are you saying?" asked Christopher.

"I don't know," she replied. "I'm not sure what I'm saying."

"Erinos is still a perfect world, isn't it?"

"But we didn't make it that way," said Kysha. "The Overseers did. They instructed us. They told us what to do and taught us how to be. We don't decide for ourselves. We obey the Overseers and obey the Life Laws and we have no choice. The only real choice I have ever made in my whole life was to leave with Ben-Harran."

"And then you were free," Ben-Harran concluded. "You were free to act from your own will and no longer controlled by the Overseers."

"Yes," said Kysha. Then she paused. "What do you mean?"

Ben-Harran smiled.

Those satellites that orbited Erinos were not there merely to control the weather, he said. They also transmitted high-frequency vibrations, a subliminal music that soothed the human mind and affected the neocortex of the brain. Under its influence people were lulled into a state of nonaggression and their creative-inventive-imaginative faculties failed to function. Thus they accepted whatever ideas were fed to them by the Overseers and obeyed the Life Laws without questioning. All but a few who were immune, who were taken to Atui and persuaded to cooperate of their own free will and returned to Erinos as the Changed Ones. Or, if they did not agree to cooperate, they were taken elsewhere, to a planet beyond the rim of the universe and left to live as they would.

Listening, Kysha felt her mind grow numb, unable to absorb what she heard, unable to believe it. On the great vision screen that had once been a wall, the ship landed in a shock of silence, although the music of Erinos still played around her. There were the willows growing by the river and the meadow grass shining unbearably bright, not green but golden. But everything she knew, and everything she saw, and all she had ever trusted, had been destroyed.

"But that's diabolical!" said Christopher.

"It's called socioevolutionary programming," said Ben-Harran. "Maelyn's brainchild originally."

"The High Council of Atui actually approves of it?"

"It is common practice on all worlds but mine."

"But it's turning people into zombies!" said Christopher. "Whole populations . . . mentally deficient! Billions of minds being suppressed! What can they ever hope to gain?"

Ben-Harran shrugged.

"Eventually, when all individuals are intellectually advanced, the controls will be removed. Then, Atui believes, people will continue to obey the Life Laws of their own free will. Control will then mean self-control and the perfection of all worlds will be by general consensus."

"Will it work?" asked Christopher.

"Try asking Kysha," Ben-Harran suggested.

That was why she had been brought to Ben-Harran's castle, as a specimen, an example, proving Maelyn's scheme of planetary control was a fallacy. Remove the controls and people would degenerate, just as she had. Those parts of their minds, suppressed and unused, would start to awaken, give rise to thoughts and feelings never experienced before, troubling and terrible and not understood. They would cope with them no better than she had. All the little grievances and jealousies, all the hurts inflicted in a few careless words, would build up and build up and finally explode. A perfect child of a perfect world Kysha might have been, but she had not stayed perfect for long. And neither would Erinos.

A huge rage filled her. The Changed Ones, the Overseers, the High Council of Atui, had deprived her of the powers of her own mind, stripped her of her curiosity, her right to choose, her right to decide, a chance to learn from her own experience. Now, with no one to teach her and no one to explain, she was almost incapable of understanding anything or anyone, including herself, unable to deduce or imagine or work things out. She was mentally deficient, just as Christopher said.

He touched her arm.

"I'm sorry," he said huskily. "I didn't understand."

Her anger grew wild and she lost control.

"How dare they!" she shrieked. "How dare they do that to me! They have no right! No right to set themselves up and rule the universe! No right to control people's minds! I hate them—Maelyn and the High Council. They are monstrous and evil!"

Her clenched fist smashed on the control console. And the music played on, the music of Erinos, a beautiful, peaceful, unforgivable planet. She would never return there. She never wanted to return. She could never belong with her family again—Dev, her mother, her father, unquestioning people, never knowing themselves. She was glad Ben-Harran had come and chosen her and taken her away, glad to be here in this castle. She had smashed up Mahri's room and he had let her, and she was glad of that too. She had learned from it, learned the difference between right and wrong, learned for herself from her own actions, gained from a freedom she had always been denied. She wanted to thank him but she did not know how. She simply turned to him with all her anger.

"Can't you stop them?" she demanded.

CHAPTER 9

L INEAR TRAVEL is necessary in a three-dimensional universe, but in Atui the surest way to arrive was by mind travel. Maelyn had merely to envision a person or a place and desire to be there. It was not far, in the grounds of the Administration building, a small secret garden surrounded by high walls. The woven carpets and the pale walls of her apartment faded into fallen petals on a gravel path, and the twitterings of the Quorm were replaced by bird songs. For a while, at least, Maelyn had escaped the detestable machine.

She breathed in the sweetness. Under a sky that was no sky but just a brightness, the colors glowed—yellow sun vines, crimson roses, waterlilies waxen white. Every flower, every leaf, every blade of grass was haloed with light, little glowing auras around all things—flies and day moths and each small facet of gravel shining with its own existence. On Atui all worlds were shadows. And genocide seemed irrelevant there, the very thought of it irreverent, yet think of it she must. It was why she had come there, seeking quietness and solitude, absence from the Quorm's perpetual arguings, its insistence that she should change her charge.

And should I? she mused.

No. Ben-Harran is guilty and everyone knows it.

But can I prove deliberate intent?

No, she admitted. *I can't, of course. So the Quorm is right, damn it! I am bound to alter the charge.*

But to what?

Of what do I accuse Ben-Harran now?

What is the real issue?

She sighed deeply, stared into the depths of the pool. Among shadows of the lily leaves, the fish moved in quicksilver gleams, true to their natures as human beings seldom were in the universe outside Atui. Souls bound in flesh, they seemed incapable of evolving to the point where control and supervision became unnecessary. Uncontrolled, unsupervised, they simply ran amok, destroyed their environment, extinguished other life forms or enslaved and slaughtered each other. No Galactic Controller would willingly let that happen, nor could the High Council allow it. Yet Ben-Harran condoned it, seeing the ghastly mayhem of worlds as learning devices, testing grounds from which true intelligence sprang. For all the deaths and disasters he had no pity.

He had proved himself heartless, Maelyn thought bitterly, proved himself inhuman and uncaring. He could not be allowed to continue. Perhaps she should study the transcripts of that previous trial, note the list of former charges and Luanna's argument that had found Ben-Harran guilty? Or maybe seek her advice?

Automatically the thought triggered the desire, formed an image in Maelyn's mind and sought its target, touched Luanna with a tug of knowledge that someone, somewhere, required an audience. She was not obliged to respond. Had she been otherwise occupied or unwilling, she had merely to dismiss the idea and break the mental link. Instead she accepted the thought, recognized Maelyn and allowed herself to be drawn toward her through the ether.

And so Luanna appeared beside the lily pond, insubstantial at first, just the brilliant green of her aura around the white core of her being, coalescing into shape and form as Maelyn watched—a woman wearing a blue gown, tall and stately, with gold braided hair coiled around her head. Gray eyes that could be as cold and hard as flint smiled in greeting.

"How can I help you?" she said.

"It is I who should have come to you," Maelyn replied.

"No matter," said Luanna. "A respite from duty is sometimes welcome, and this is a beautiful place."

"I wish to consult you," said Maelyn.

"About what?" asked Luanna.

"Ben-Harran," said Maelyn. "The Quorm has advised me I should change the charge."

Luanna frowned. "It would be safer, of course. We need a guaranteed result."

"The indictments you made before?"

"Cannot apply now," said Luanna.

"So what do you suggest?"

Luanna frowned again.

Her gray eyes narrowed against the light.

"I suppose we are back to the great debate," she said wearily. "Ben-Harran will challenge us yet again as to our right to control the worlds we rule. In his exile he has had time enough in a single galaxy to prove the error of our ways. Instead, with the destruction of Zeeda, he has proved the error of his. He is not fit to hold the position of Galactic Controller. Why not charge him with dereliction of duty or culpable negligence?"

"On what criteria?" Maelyn inquired.

"Our own, of course," said Luanna.

"And are we so convinced we are right?"

"Do you doubt the methods you yourself introduced?"

"I question them," Maelyn admitted. "Surely we all do?"

"But not our motives," said Luanna.

"Oh no," said Maelyn. "They are beyond doubt."

"And there is your conviction," said Luanna. "On that you base your argument, on that you answer any countercharge Ben-Harran may throw at us."

"And for that I thank you," said Maelyn.

The older woman smiled and nodded and her form faded, leaving only the yellow brightness of the air, a flutter of leaves in an unseen wind and the soft twittering of a bird. Or was it? Furiously Maelyn turned to face the Quorm, which was hovering among the roses, an aerial spy arrived unnoticed to witness the weakness of her uncertainty. Its audio antennae quivered delicately and its silver body pulsed.

"How long have you been there?" Maelyn asked angrily.

"In linear time?" inquired the Quorm.

"Eavesdropping!" said Maelyn. "In terms of duration!"

"Five minutes and twenty-three seconds," trilled the Quorm.

"And how did you find me?"

Eyes on stalks regarded her.

"Had you studied my manufacturer's instructions," it said, "you would have noted that I am sensitive to all personal vibrational patterns and am able to trace them within a given radius."

"And if I had studied your manufacturer's instructions, would I have found any reference to your ability to respect personal privacy?" Maelyn asked curtly. "A grievous omission,

I suspect. However, as you have already overheard, Lady Luanna agreed with your advice and I have decided to accept it. Ben-Harran will be charged with culpable negligence, and proceedings will begin as soon as he presents himself. So you can home in on the personal vibrations of the Control Room Supervisor and request him to relay that information to whoever is on the receiving end in Ben-Harran's castle."

"Excuse me," began the Quorm.

Maelyn raised her hands.

Blue light flickered at her fingertips and her blue eyes flashed.

"No!" she said. "Not anymore! If I hear one more 'excuse me' from you, I shall reduce you to a ball bearing!"

CHAPTER 10

CHRISTOPHER WATCHED helplessly as Kysha beat with her fists on the control panel. He could understand how she felt. He was as appalled as she was, although he was not personally affected. It was like hearing tales of repressive governments on Earth, or watching the television coverage of famine in Africa, military atrocities or the plight of the Vietnamese boat people. He knew it was terrible, that it should not be allowed to happen, but as an individual, he could do nothing about it. And there was nothing he could do about Erinos either, only be thankful he had not been born there.

Staring at the vision screen that had once been a wall, at the green-brown world so perfectly conceived, Christopher felt an overwhelming sadness. If only, he thought, they could have achieved it in some other way, through the wisdom, common sense and cooperation of the majority of its inhabitants, then he could have conceded the rule of Atui was right. Instead, he was beginning to side with Ben-Harran. And that was like trusting a volcano, aware that at any moment Ben-Harran might explode. Kysha must have sensed that same potential, for suddenly she turned, appealed to Ben-Harran with all her anger.

"Can't you stop them?" she demanded.

He could, thought Christopher.

Unleashed, Ben-Harran could blast the High Council of Atui out of existence and rule the universe himself if he so wished. But it seemed he was not to be tempted.

"I have no voice in Atui," he replied. "Over this very issue I rebelled and lost my place. Now I am just a Galactic Controller, and I have little hope of persuading the High Council to abandon their methods for an even more terrible alternative."

"What can be more terrible than a world where all people's minds are controlled?" Kysha asked furiously.

Christopher sighed, sensed what was coming.

"A world where people's minds are not controlled, perhaps? Somewhere like Earth?"

"Or Herra-Venda," said Mahri.

Christopher turned his head.

She was a dark shape on the threshold of the control room, the Erg Unit beside her, its eyes glowing green, its limbs reflecting the sunlight of Erinos in silvery gleams. A peculiar association, thought Christopher. Not long ago the Erg Unit would have steered clear of Mahri, calculating from its own experiences that she was dangerous. Now, since Ben-Harran had adjusted its situation-assessment programming, it must have reassessed her and reversed its responses.

Unless Mahri herself had changed? In the dim light coming from the vision screen, it was hard to be sure. All Christopher could see was the wild frizz of her hair and a silken glimmer of clothing as she approached. Her limp remained, and she leaned on the Erg Unit's arm for support. But at least she had changed her dress, thought Christopher, and her voice sounded unusually civil.

"We have done as you asked," she informed Ben-Harran.

"Then join us, my lady," Ben-Harran replied.

He rose from the chair.

The Erg Unit's feet clattered noisily across the floor.

And Kysha muttered, "We don't want *her* in here!"

"Why not?" asked Christopher.

"Because she's vicious and stupid and she understands nothing!"

"So don't begrudge her the chance to learn," he urged her.

Kysha became silent, thinking things over.

"I'm sorry," she murmured. "I didn't mean what I said."

But she had, thought Christopher.

And Mahri had learned already, it seemed.

On Ben-Harran's instructions, she had let the Erg Unit teach her. She had learned about the workings of the universe, how stars were suns, and one, light years away, had Herra-Venda orbiting around it. She had learned about Atui and the High Council, how most worlds were controlled. But Ben-Harran's were not, and for that failure, he was accused. Guilty, the Erg Unit had informed her, for the destruction of a planet and the extinction of millions of life forms, crimes he had not committed and for which he was not responsible.

"You can be so certain?" Ben-Harran asked her.

"Would you rather I doubted you?" Mahri replied.

"Who cares what you think!" muttered Kysha.

Music played softly, the life forms of Erinos singing their existence, yet Ben-Harran heard. His black eyes flashed as he turned toward her.

"*I* care!" Ben-Harran informed her. "I care what each of you thinks, even the Erg Unit."

"Why?" Christopher asked impulsively. "Why should you care what any of us thinks?"

"Yes," said Kysha. "Why should you care, Ben-Harran? We're just specimens to you . . . and stupid as well!"

"That," said Ben-Harran, "is a judgment. And that is exactly what I require from you—the judgment of your thoughts . . . before I take the stand, face the High Council of Atui and make my plea. You are both very quick to judge yourselves and each other, so now you may judge me."

Christopher stared at him in alarm.

"I don't think I'm qualified."

"That is another self-judgment."

"Then we would prefer not to," said Kysha.

"The fate of this galaxy may depend upon you."

"I don't see how . . ." Christopher began.

"You will," Ben-Harran promised him.

The control room plunged into darkness and silence, and the weight of worlds fell on Christopher's mind. And maybe Kysha shared it—feelings of trepidation and reluctance. Her hand sought his, clutched and clung, and he could feel her trembling.

*   *   *

Once more the nebula sang in a symphony of color. Once more the shift of speed, the shriek of sound, the streaking corridor of stairs. Once more the slow approach to a star system, a world singled out like a turquoise jewel spinning toward him. It might have been Earth, thought Christopher, except for the dozen tiny moons that revolved around it. And when the music changed, he did not need to go there to know what it was like. He could imagine from the sound of it, a barrage of noise, a ghastly discordancy that caused Kysha to pull away from him and cover her ears with her hands—until Ben-Harran lowered the volume.

"Is Earth's song like this?" asked Christopher.

"Similar," Ben-Harran said grimly.

"But why?" asked Kysha. "Why is it so horrible?"

"In a moment you will see why," Ben-Harran told her.

"And do we travel with the castle?" asked Mahri.

"It's a video recording," Kysha said crushingly.

"What is video?" asked Mahri.

"I can explain," droned the Erg Unit.

"Later," Ben-Harran said curtly.

"Elucidation is necessary, master," the Erg Unit replied.

"And you are here for your own elucidation, Erg Unit! So watch! Listen! And learn!"

The Erg Unit complied.

Space and stars faded into cerulean-blue skies as the ship dropped lower. Lower still and the sunlight gave way to massed cloud that slowly cleared to reveal the blue shimmer of the sea and the outline of an unknown continent beneath. Christopher saw brown desert regions and matte green forests and snowcapped mountains in the distance. Then minute patches of farmlands, gray squares of cities, pinpoints of fire among tiny billows of black smoke.

"What's that?" he asked.

"Later," said Ben-Harran. "Right now we go no nearer."

"So how can we see?" asked Kysha.

"Magnification three point five," Ben-Harran murmured.

The sudden shift made Christopher feel sick. He clutched the control panel as the scanners zoomed toward the planet's surface and skimmed across a cornfield. Or maybe it was a prairie, a vast treeless plain where no other life existed, not even a bird, just the electricity pylons striding across it and an army of huge machines eating their way into it. Monocul-ture, he thought, and chemically dependent. Then came miles of storage silos where trucks unloaded, bald concrete roadways and a gaunt gray village of prefabricated houses built around a railway terminal. The scanners followed the tracks past endless acres of greenhouses, more prefabricated villages and endless acres of covered sheds.

"Factory farming," Ben-Harran said.

"What's that?" asked Kysha.

"Explain to her, Christopher," Ben-Harran said.

Christopher sighed. He knew full well what Kysha's reac-tion would be and was reluctant to tell her—the sheds housed birds and animals reared for slaughter, millions upon millions of living creatures who never saw the light of day. They were butchered for meat, and the carcasses were car-ried by refrigerated wagons to be sold in the shops to the millions upon millions of people who lived in the cities.

"They eat them," said Christopher.

In the semidarkness Kysha stared at him.

"You mean they're all carnivores on this planet?"

"Omnivores, probably, as we are on Earth."

"And so many of them," Ben-Harran remarked. "Like a plague of locusts they eat their planet bare and they control neither their habits nor their breeding potential."

"Why do the Overseers allow it?" Kysha demanded.

"I don't employ Overseers," Ben-Harran reminded her.

"You mean this is one of your hell worlds?" Kysha shud-dered.

In the reflected light, her eyes were wide with loathing, and all over again she would hate him, Christopher thought. The music played on, dreary, unmelodic, grating on his nerves—a world singing of garbage dumps and power stations belching smoke, fumes from a chemical plant drifting across a polluted landscape and highways jammed with cars.

Vaguely, Christopher heard Ben-Harran explain the use and significance of the internal combustion engine, but he paid little heed. He gazed instead at a shantytown of tin shacks built on an area of wasteland, at starving children searching through garbage dumps for scraps, at a bleak compound that housed the unwanted dregs of that inhuman society—the criminal, or the homeless, or the insane. There must have been thousands crammed inside, a milling mass of people, hands reaching through the wire mesh, begging and imploring as the cars swept past. Armed guards dragged out the dead.

"I don't want to see any more," whimpered Kysha.

Christopher could do nothing to console her, nothing to soften the reality of what she was seeing. Relentlessly the scanners swept on over the industrial environs of a city where litter blew in the wind and the air was a murk of fog and fumes and smoke. What few pedestrians there were wore protective masks, and trees were leafless skeletons, grass sere and brown in public parks.

Then, among canyons of streets, between skyscraper blocks of offices and flats, the neon signs flashed. And it might have been Earth Christopher was gazing at . . . New York, Hong Kong, Tokyo or London. It was so ugly, wept Kysha, so grim and dirty and colorless. And all those people imprisoned there! He tried to tell her they were not imprisoned but were there of their own free will, men and women choosing to work there. But his voice had a hollow ring and he failed to convince even himself. Given a choice, no one in his right mind would choose to work in that particular city—so either they were all crazy or they had no choice. Slaves of a system probably, he thought, with no alternative and no escape, stymied from birth as most people were on Earth.

And whose fault was it? he wondered.

Who was responsible?

"God forbid the future of Herra-Venda should be like this," murmured Mahri.

* * *

It had nothing to do with God, thought Christopher. God was the great creative force that flowed through the universe, through all living things and all human minds, the power Ben-Harran allowed and Atui denied. Yet there was no evidence of God on this planet, no beauty, no art, nothing fine or uplifting or life enhancing. But then he saw that there was. For on the far side of the city the scenery changed.

Here were remnants of an older culture. Trees, not totally dead from pollution, lined sweeping avenues, and in the gardens of grand houses a few hardy shrubs and flowers continued to survive. Christopher saw great public buildings, theaters and amphitheaters, triumphal arches, vast open squares with monuments and fountains. But the stonework was blackened and crumbling, faces of statues eroded away, and scaffolding surrounded the tapering towers of what could only be a cathedral.

Kysha sniffed and wiped her eyes.

"What's that place?" she asked.

"A center of worship," Ben-Harran replied.

"I don't understand worship."

"It is ritual service conducted by priests," Mahri explained. "They kneel before their God, chant formal words and beg for favors and mercy."

"You are a cynic, lady," Ben-Harran said softly.

"And what does God mean?" asked Kysha.

"Christopher?" said Ben-Harran. "What does God mean to you?"

It was as if he had read Christopher's mind and knew his thoughts. But defining the undefinable to someone who had no conception of any divine presence was not easy. God was the creator of the universe, the source of the Life Laws, he said.

"You mean the High Council of Atui?" asked Kysha.

"Not just them," said Christopher. "You, me, and everything else as well—a slug or a star or a lettuce leaf—the spiritual essence of things. I don't know what God is. It's whatever you revere, or love, or respect."

"But the inhabitants of that planet don't respect anything, do they?"

"If it's like Earth," said Christopher, "they respect lots of things—power and money and material goods, winning, status."

"So are they evil or stupid?" asked Kysha.

"Many may be wise and kind," Mahri said gently.

"I don't see any evidence of that!" Kysha retorted.

"If I were to separate the strands of sound and focus on the musical vibrations of individuals, you would certainly hear them," Ben-Harran informed her.

But they were ineffectual, thought Christopher, like players in an orchestra where most were out of tune and the conductor was insane. What use were a few violins playing perfectly amid the general din? They did not alter the overall effect, the song of the planet that sickened and repelled.

Then the landscape softened and the city faded to a spacious suburbia that faded in turn to an expanse of blue inland water reflecting the sky. Here were plush yachts and speedboats, open-air restaurants, and sumptuous dwellings along the wooded shores.

Christopher heard the incredulity in Kysha's voice.

"How can those people live like that when others are starving?"

"They probably don't even think about it," said Christopher.

"You mean they don't care?"

"Not enough to give up any portion of what they have."

"Why doesn't someone make them?"

"Who?" asked Christopher. "That's the order of things. Whoever rules favors the few, and the rest make do with what little they can get."

"That's what I did," said Mahri.

"Queen of the High Plains," Kysha said sourly.

"Daughter of a king," said Mahri. "And that gave me the right to rule the tribe, or so I thought. Those who supported me I rewarded and those who opposed me died. And to all who slaved and served, I spared hardly a thought but accepted it, as they did, as their lot in life. Those were my crimes. But I cannot answer for the crimes of my lieutenants and sublieutenants, for the cook who whipped the pot boy and the pot boy who whipped the dog."

Kysha sniffed. "Is there some point to that?"

"I think she means we're all responsible for how we behave no matter who rules us," said Christopher.

"Well, that's obvious!" said Kysha.

"Is it?" Ben-Harran said quietly. "Do you truly believe it, Kysha? And will you even remember it when you see what happens next?"

He touched the controls.

The scanner of his ship fast-forwarded, sped across a range of mountains to a vast dustbowl of desert, slowed and steadied to reveal an army on the march, convoys of trucks, regiments of tanks, heavy artillery and missile launchers. Christopher was unsurprised. War on such a world was almost as inevitable as it was on Earth. Shells streaked through the sunlight and he watched, dispassionately, a city being bombarded, blasted buildings and billowings of smoke and fire. Then, quite suddenly, everything ended in a flash of searing light and the slow terrible forming of a mushroom-shaped cloud. Atomics, he thought, a nuclear explosion, some kind of holocaust about to happen.

"What are they doing?" shrieked Kysha.

"Waging war," Christopher told her.

"They'll be destroyed!" cried Kysha. "They'll all be destroyed!"

"That's the intention," Christopher said brutally.

"Don't let me see!" wailed Kysha. "I don't want to see!"

She turned toward Christopher, hid her face against him, and he put his arms around her. But he could not protect her from what was happening.

The scanners drew back and Ben-Harran's ship retreated. A shriek of insane music filled the control room. And as the bombs went on falling, the sky ignited; the atmosphere caught fire. Mahri gasped in horror and unashamedly Kysha wept, but Christopher felt nothing. He had seen it too often in films and on television to be touched by it. It was like a scene from a space fantasy, almost unreal, good effects but a lousy story line, no hero or heroine, no human being with whom he could identify and get involved. He simply watched—a planet burning, millions of life forms dying.

And the song of it faded until nothing remained but a murmuring of molecules amid a background of stars.

The control room snapped into darkness.

"That was Zeeda," Ben-Harran said.

*   *   *

There was nothing to say, thought Christopher. Like a movie audience at the end of a film, they waited for the lights to come on. It was happening already. Magically, and from no source, came a predawn gloom that slowly intensified, stunning his eyes, dulling Ben-Harran's aura and gleaming on Kysha's tears as he released her. Christopher could imagine how she felt, violated by visions of inhumanity undreamed of on Erinos. But he had grown up with it, watched it almost daily on television news reports and violent entertainment programs. He was overexposed to atrocity and almost indifferent to it. Given a choice, he would have liked to return to his room, play his guitar for an hour or so, then sleep and forget. But from the control room of Ben-Harran's castle and the white light shining there was no escape. Amid the soft sounds of Kysha sobbing, the creak of the Erg Unit's limbs and Mahri's breath, Christopher watched Ben-Harran pace the shining floor. His black robes sparked with static, and fire licked his heels as he turned. His eyes that raked their faces seemed sharp as claws.

"Well?" he demanded. "You have judged me before for good or ill, and you are quick enough to judge each other. Why now do you hesitate? Am I to blame for the death of that world? Am I guilty, as Maelyn claims? Or can you, from your own knowledge of the facts, reach an independent conclusion?"

It seemed obvious to Christopher that Ben-Harran was not guilty. Zeeda had destroyed itself. But why, he wondered, should Maelyn accuse Ben-Harran of something he had not done? She was not like Christopher, prepared to believe his own suspicions for want of a better explanation. She was a member of the High Council of Atui with access to the facts. She had to know Ben-Harran had not fired those warheads, so why had she told the Erg Unit he was guilty of genocide? Why was he on trial at all? Christopher was about to ask when Ben-Harran picked on the Erg Unit.

"You, Erg Unit—what do you say?"

"I . . ." it droned. "I am a machine, master."

"Is that an excuse?"

"I cannot judge or form opinions."

"Why so?" Ben-Harran asked it. "You have a mind, do you not? An intelligence capable of logical thought? Use it, Erg Unit. Refer to your latest situation-assessment programming and give me your opinion."

Light shone on the Erg Unit's silver limbs.

Its eyes burned green, and its voice was strangely hesitant.

"I . . ." it droned.

"Yes?" prompted Ben-Harran.

"If I assess the situation, it is illogical, master."

"Why?" said Ben-Harran.

"There is evidence of two conflicting premises," said the Erg Unit.

"State them," Ben-Harran commanded.

"All individuals must be free to develop according to the dictates of their consciences," said the Erg Unit. "They must be free to test the validity of all given laws . . . and they are responsible for their own actions. That is your belief, master. According to it, you are not guilty for the destruction of Zeeda."

"And the opposing premise?" Ben-Harran inquired.

"Yes," said the Erg Unit. "Atui believes that individuals cannot be allowed to develop according to their inclinations because they are not sufficiently evolved to assume responsibility for their actions. Planetary control is therefore necessary, and responsibility lies with the Galactic Controller. According to Atui you *are* guilty for the destruction of Zeeda."

"And what do *you* conclude?" Ben-Harran asked it.

"If you are not guilty, you cannot be guilty," the Erg Unit said. "And if you are guilty, you cannot be not guilty. Paradoxical situations are insoluble. I cannot compute."

Ben-Harran shook his head.

"Both beliefs cannot be right, Erg Unit. They contradict each other. Therefore, you must choose one on which to base your judgment and reject the other."

The Erg Unit's eyes blazed brighter.

"I am a machine," it said. "I cannot . . ."

"You cannot refuse to obey me," said Ben-Harran.

"No," agreed the Erg Unit. "I cannot refuse. I must choose. You are not guilty. You are guilty. Both judgments cannot be correct. I must choose . . . I must . . . I cannot . . . I . . . er . . ."

Its voice wound down. Its eyes pulsed emerald green, flashed and went out. Its internal mechanism whirred and clicked and stopped. Its metal arms hung limply at its sides. Turned off inside, it settled into stillness, silence, its own little death.

"Now we know the real issue," Ben-Harran announced.

Christopher felt confused. It was not as simple as he had thought. At the back of Maelyn's accusation was the question of moral responsibility. And unlike the Erg Unit, Christopher could not escape from the interrogation or avoid making a decision. It seemed to him, then, that it was he and Kysha and Mahri who were about to go on trial, not Ben-Harran.

*　　*　　*

Nervously, Christopher chewed his lip as Ben-Harran prowled and waited, catlike, predatory, about to pounce. And the old terror returned to prey on him, gripped his stomach, dried his throat, paralyzed his mind. He had no choice but to face it and overcome it or remain forever as he was—timorous and intimidated, afraid to speak out in case he was wrong, as obedient as the Erg Unit to all authority, however restricting, belittling or questionable.

He realized then that this was the challenge Ben-Harran had represented right from the beginning. He had invited Christopher to step from a state of fear and powerlessness and meet him on equal terms. All along Christopher's own mind had fought to dissuade him, refusing to discriminate between truth and fabrication, making an enemy of a being who had probably saved his life. He had never really given Ben-Harran a chance. But he could now, of his own free will. All it took was courage and the effort to assert himself, a clenched fist, a deep breath, a human voice.

"I don't think you're guilty," said Christopher.

Ben-Harran halted and turned slowly to face him. Christopher had almost expected him to be grateful, but instead, the black eyes glittered, and behind them was all the power and darkness of a mind about to strike. The terror rose and pitched within him. He saw death, destruction, a moment that might be eternal, blotting him out like a snuffed candle. Then he was empty of emotion. There was nothing inside him but an ocean of calm and quiet and stillness in which he floated and the vast shining spaces of the room around him.

What flowed through the silence between him and Ben-Harran was hard to define . . . recognition, perhaps, or understanding. He knew only that Ben-Harran knew him in a way he did not even know himself, and for just a few fractions of a second he knew Ben-Harran. Yes, he was ruthless and remorseless, but his respect for all people and all life was absolute and he cared with an integrity that would never be swayed, not even for pity. Christopher might sweat with his own temerity, but he need never fear him again. Very slightly, as if in acknowledgment, Ben-Harran inclined his head.

"You were saying?"

"I don't think you're guilty," Christopher repeated.

"But how reliable is your thinking?" Ben-Harran asked him.

Christopher hesitated.

He had been wrong from the start about Ben-Harran.

But this time he was certain of something.

"You didn't fire those nuclear warheads," he said, "so technically, at least, you can't possibly be found guilty of genocide."

"Oh come," said Ben-Harran. "Maelyn will not let me slip from her hands over a mere technicality. She will change her charge. Genocide is not the main issue. What happened on Zeeda is a matter of cause and effect, and I, according to Maelyn's beliefs, am that cause."

"Zeeda destroyed itself," argued Christopher.

"So I am not responsible?" said Ben-Harran. "Even though I could have stopped it?"

Christopher regarded him uncertainly.

"What do you mean?"

"I could have stopped it," Ben-Harran repeated. "I could

have sent in Overseers long ago, set up a system of satellites, taken over, ruled as Atui rules."

"So why didn't you?" Christopher asked him.

"Why indeed?" Ben-Harran replied.

Again, Christopher hesitated.

This time he looked to Kysha to support him, although he guessed she would not. She had lived all her life under the rule of the Overseers, and now that she had escaped, she was hardly likely to advocate it for any other world. He was alone with his opinion, able to see no other option. Untold billions of human lives were at stake, and in spite of his reluctance he had no choice but to oppose Ben-Harran.

"When someone's drowning," he said, "you don't just watch them, you throw them a lifeline. You must have known they had nuclear weapons on Zeeda and you must have known they were on the brink of war. You must also have known that spontaneous combustion of the atmosphere is a possible result. I mean, we know that much on Earth."

"Exactly," said Ben-Harran. "You know it on Earth and they knew it on Zeeda. And, given free will, the intelligence to use it and the capacity to assess the likely consequences of their actions, I credit the inhabitants of all my planets with sense enough not to commit the ultimate folly of self-destruction."

"So you goofed," said Christopher.

"My confidence in the inhabitants of Zeeda was somewhat misplaced," Ben-Harran admitted. "An unfortunate oversight on my part perhaps, but I do not claim to be omniscient."

"So what about Earth?" asked Christopher.

"What about it?" Ben-Harran inquired.

"The same thing could happen there, couldn't it? And if

we don't blow ourselves up, we could die from pollution or starvation, overpopulation or lack of resources."

"Is that my responsibility?" Ben-Harran said indifferently.

Suddenly, unexpectedly, Kysha took Christopher's side in the argument.

"How can it not be your responsibility!" she said angrily. "You're the Galactic Controller, Ben-Harran! You're responsible for everything that happens on every world that is yours! And it wasn't the death of Zeeda that was so terrible but the life of it—all those starving people, all that greed and selfishness and despoliation, the sick, rotten social system! It was a hell world, just as Maelyn said. And you let it be like that! You allowed it! And if Earth is the same as Zeeda, you cannot go on allowing it, not if you have any pity!"

Christopher glanced at her. She had moved to stand beside him, his ally against all odds, pale and shaking with emotion. But her blue eyes blazed. She had never been afraid to face the Galactic Controller.

"What do you suggest I do?" Ben-Harran asked her.

"You know what you must do!" Kysha said fiercely.

"Control people's minds? Deprive them of freedom? All that was done to you, Kysha? Can you really countenance that?"

"Yes!" said Kysha. "Because now I know why!"

"People don't want freedom," said Christopher.

"Do you have evidence to support that claim?" Ben-Harran asked him.

The evidence was there on Earth.

"Freedom means responsibility," Christopher went on. "And who wants to be responsible for the mess we've made on Earth? No one, Ben-Harran! Given a choice, we vote away our freedom, elect governments to be responsible for us, choose to be ruled. So we may as well be ruled by Atui and the Overseers. At least *they* care about all people equally, create a just society and ensure the survival of the planet."

Ben-Harran stared at him.

"Is that what you truly advocate, Christopher? A world where the creative imagination can have no place? A world without art, or music, or literature?"

"And no nuclear weapons either!" Christopher retorted. "What loss is the *Moonlight Sonata* or the Mona Lisa compared to the salvation of a world?"

"He's right!" Kysha said fiercely.

Ben-Harran nodded and turned to Mahri.

"What say you, lady?"

She was a presence Christopher had forgotten, a warrior woman in a brown satin gown ripped at the seams and fastened by a brooch at one shoulder. Once he had admired her in her savagery, but now that fierce yellow beauty was gone from her eyes and her looks were marred by the puckered scar on her face. Unshed tears shone in her eyes, and she winced with pain as she struggled to her feet. All but her life Ben-Harran had taken from her. And more than Christopher or Kysha, Mahri had reason to hate him. But her words surprised him.

"How do you bear it?" she asked. "How do you bear our human stupidity? All those millions and millions of foolish little lives?"

"Because I must," Ben-Harran informed her.

"And so must we," mourned Mahri. "We must bear what we are and learn from it and continue until we grow wise. There is no other way, is there? And no room for pity. For whoever binds us to obey whatever law is a tyrant, however benign."

"And you should know!" Kysha said furiously. "If there were Overseers on Herra-Venda, then the likes of you would not exist! And hundreds or thousands of people would have escaped *your* tyranny!"

Christopher frowned in a moment of uncertainty, but what meaning he gleaned from Mahri's words vanished from his head. Suddenly, in Ben-Harran's castle, the alarm system switched itself on. Bells rang and a siren wailed, and on the far side of the control room came a huge crack of sound. They were under attack, thought Christopher. Kysha screamed as the wall split open, like a broken window letting through a blaze of yellow light. Just for a moment Christopher thought he saw another control room, similar to this but a thousand times more vast, where men and women wearing white uniforms stared at him in surprise. Then, hurtling through the space-time barrier, came something round and silver, a huge ball bearing or a bouncing bomb aimed straight at Christopher's head.

CHAPTER 11

THE THING CAME THROUGH the wall and Kysha screamed
in terror, saw Christopher duck and Mahri pick up the
guitar, aim it to strike—until Ben-Harran stayed her arm.
The projectile hurtled past, struck the opposite wall and fell
with a clatter, rolled across the shining floor toward her and
lay still. Kysha had been wild with fury a moment ago, hating
Mahri and hating Ben-Harran, but now she turned to him.

"What is it?" she asked.

Christopher gripped her wrist, pulled her away.

"It's a bomb!" he said.

"Shall I hurl it back?" asked Mahri.

"Leave it where it is," Ben-Harran requested.

"If it explodes we'll all be killed!" Christopher said urgently.

Ben-Harran smiled. "Atui would never deal in explosive
devices," he said.

Kysha stared at it suspiciously, an inert ball of silvery metal.
Or maybe it was not inert? Something pulsed within it, liquid
or light beating like a heart, red brightening to gold. Then it
stirred, sprouted arms and tripod legs and a pair of antennae,

rose like a giant insect and hopped a few paces nearer. Once again Christopher urged her away, increasing her fear. It was some kind of robotic device, she thought, sent there for a purpose. To control her mind, maybe, and reverse the process Ben-Harran had begun. Computerized circuits burbled and hummed, and eyes on thin stalks twitched delicate as a snail's. Then, in a small shrill voice, the thing spoke.

"Excuse me," it said, "but is this Ben-Harran's castle?"

"It is," Ben-Harran replied gravely.

"In that case," said the thing, "I claim political asylum."

There was a moment of surprised silence.

Then Christopher laughed and released Kysha's wrist.

"Is it for real?" he asked.

"I do believe it is," Ben-Harran replied.

"So what is it?" Kysha repeated.

"I'm a Quorm," said the thing. "A Quantizing and Omni-Reasoning Module, the only one of my kind."

"So they finally invented you," Ben-Harran murmured.

"Oh yes," said the Quorm. "They invented me. But I am not appreciated. My intelligence irritates and my continuing existence could well be at risk if I remain in Atui. I have been threatened with extinction, you know."

"So you have come to me to save your life," Ben-Harran concluded.

"I could be very useful to you," the Quorm said earnestly.

"How did you get here?" Ben-Harran asked it.

"We saw," said Mahri. "It came through the wall."

"Through the space-time interface barrier," said Christopher.

"But I put a lock on it," said Ben-Harran. "One way only. Out from my castle but never in."

"I reversed it," the Quorm said proudly.

"Remarkable," said Ben-Harran. "Your intelligence astounds me. What has foiled Atui for centuries has been solved in seconds by a single Quorm. You used their computers, I presume? And do the data banks retain your instructions?"

"Well yes," said the Quorm. "Information cannot be canceled or modified without the sequencer code, which, as of yet, I have been unable to ascertain."

"So Atui has only to repeat your procedure?"

There was another, different, silence.

"Oh dear!" wailed the Quorm. "What have I done?"

"What indeed?" Ben-Harran replied. "Your political asylum could be very short-lived, my friend."

Kysha glanced toward the wall. Soon the door would open in a blaze of light and beings in white clothes, like the Overseers of Erinos, would come marching through. They would take Ben-Harran captive and have him stand trial before the High Council. It was what he deserved, she thought viciously. But the Quorm seemed distraught.

"What's going to happen to me?" it cried. "I shall be hauled back to Atui and turned into a ball bearing! Or else I shall be reprogrammed, my ability to act of my own free will altered to blind obedience. My capacity to disagree wiped from my circuits. My self-expression denied. I shall be no more advanced than an Erg Unit when Maelyn is done!"

"You and billions of human beings," Ben-Harran replied.

"Don't let it happen!" begged the Quorm. "I don't want to be reduced to a robot! I don't want my thought processes tampered with! My circuits full of fixed ideas! I may make mistakes in applying all my preprogrammed knowledge, but I'm willing to learn. Please save me!"

"There is nothing I can do," Ben-Harran told it.

"Why not?" asked Mahri. "Can you not keep this small

machine, Ben-Harran? Will you not give it sanctuary in your castle?"

"He can't," Christopher said somberly. "Any minute now they'll be coming for him . . . Maelyn and the High Council, following the Quorm through the doorway in the wall."

Kysha glanced at him. She heard the regret in his voice and knew he did not want it to happen.

"As I can guarantee no other freedom until I have secured my own, there is nothing I can do," Ben-Harran concluded. "My castle will provide sanctuary for no one, Mahri. I shall be gone to Atui and no longer here."

The Quorm's antennae drooped. The bright pulse of it faded to dull red, and it burbled sadly.

"If you go into Atui, Ben-Harran, you will never be free again. You will be charged with culpable negligence, and the result is guaranteed. You are found guilty before you even get there. And what will happen to me?"

Suddenly Kysha herself felt torn. The Quorm's mechanized mind was as precious as her own and she understood its fear. And however wrong she thought Ben-Harran to be, however much she deplored the massed misery he allowed to exist, the hell on Herra-Venda and Christopher's Earth, she could not wish him to be punished or imprisoned.

"You could escape," she suggested. "You could escape in your spaceship and take the Quorm with you."

The Quorm brightened visibly.

In a swirl of robes Ben-Harran turned to face her.

"How will that serve me?" he asked. "Where would I go? And what would I do? What is my own freedom worth if all other minds are enchained? Why single me out for salvation, Kysha, and disregard the rest?"

She stared at him, crushed by his questions and unable to

answer. All over Erinos he had searched for her, chosen her, brought her to his castle, set free her mind from the controls of Atui. Now, when she tried to help him in return, he rebuffed her, made her feel wrong and stupid and turned to Mahri instead.

"How do you advise me, lady?"

"To fight them in their own court," Mahri said sternly.

"And will you testify on my behalf?"

"You do not need to ask me that, Lord Ben-Harran."

Ben-Harran turned to the Quorm.

"How about you, little friend? Will you return to Atui with me and witness the worth of your own free will?"

The Quorm trembled.

"No!" it said. "I won't go back to Atui! I won't!"

It backed toward the door on its three spindly legs.

Then it took flight, zoomed into the corridor and was gone.

"It seeks to preserve itself," said Mahri.

"As do we all," said Ben-Harran.

"That's what I meant!" Kysha said angrily.

"Was it?"

Ben-Harran laughed.

Proud, mocking, his dark eyes glittered.

And his words chilled Kysha's heart.

"So . . . I will run then. Flee in my spaceship and care not a jot for worlds or people or for you either, Kysha. Atui can have you and all that is mine. I shall retire to some quiet planet and take my ease."

"That," said an icy voice from behind him, "can be arranged, Ben-Harran."

*   *   *

Maelyn stood on the threshold of the space-time interface.

Her white gown shimmered and her hair, fair as moonlight, hung to her waist. She was beautiful, thought Kysha. But her blue eyes were cold, and pale fire hovered about her, chilling the air as she stepped forward. The control room filled with the scents of frost and flowers, with an icy power that equaled Ben-Harran's own.

Kysha shivered, and moved closer to Christopher, needing his companionship. Maelyn did not set controls on the minds of people out of love or caring, but out of necessity, she thought. And out of necessity she would bring down the one who opposed her, as ruthless as Ben-Harran was, and as remorseless. She watched in silence as Maelyn snapped her fingers.

The doorway behind her filled with shadowy shapes, beings in white uniforms who filed silently past her and formed a ring around the edges of the control room. Their light sabers glowed and their auras made a circle of rainbow colors cutting off Ben-Harran's escape.

"Is this really necessary?" he asked.

"Only you can know that," Maelyn replied.

"I would have preferred to enter Atui voluntarily."

"You would have preferred to procrastinate longer, you mean?"

Ben-Harran smiled. "Did you not need the time I gave you to be clear of your charges against me? Had I accepted your accusation of genocide, I would have been free by now, for not even the High Council could convict me of that."

"Morally you are guilty of it!" Maelyn retorted.

Ben-Harran shrugged. "Your verdict, lady, precedes the trial and is therefore invalid."

Blue annoyance flickered in Maelyn's eyes.

"Would you have us observe a set procedure, Lord Ben-Harran, when you for centuries have flouted every procedure that has ever been introduced? Very well, then. I hereby formally charge you with culpable negligence, a deliberate refusal to implement the duties and responsibilities of a Galactic Controller, as laid down in the statutes. And I formally request that you return immediately to Atui to stand trial." Her white gown fluttered as she turned to the ring of guards. "Escort him!" she said.

There was a pause before movement.

Ben-Harran would not comply, thought Kysha. He believed in individual freedom no matter what happened, and he would never comply with a request that was an order. His black eyes flashed and red-gold power flickered in the darkness that surrounded him as he raised his arms. She waited for the lightning to strike from his fingertips, and Maelyn grew pale. Then the light sabers flared and the guards surrounded him. His raised arms were nothing more than a gesture of surrender, but his voice was mocking.

"No shackles, my lady? No ball and chain?"

"Don't goad me!" Maelyn snapped.

"You will trust me not to break free?"

"As I would trust myself," Maelyn retorted. "We are both of Atui and honor bound to do as we must. Take him away!"

"One moment," said Ben-Harran.

"What now?" Maelyn asked impatiently.

"I do not go alone into Atui."

Maelyn stared at him, her eyebrows arched in surprise.

"Are you telling me you have found someone willing to speak on your behalf, Ben-Harran? Someone who understands the issues and shares your stance? Who will stand firm where your own followers would not? What manner of person is he or she who can condone the death of a world and defend the cause of it before the High Council?"

Her hard blue gaze swept slowly around the control room,

rested on Christopher, lingered a moment, then moved to Kysha. Cold and sharp as lasers the eyes bored into her, holding her still, and Maelyn's thoughts moved through her mind. She was the girl from Erinos whom Ben-Harran had manipulated into leaving. She had changed, of course, turned against Atui as Changed Ones often did, but not irretrievably so. Knowing what had happened to Zeeda, knowing the life conditions on Ben-Harran's worlds, she understood the necessity for planetary control, however much she deplored it. She would, perhaps, become a good-enough teacher given training and time. Maelyn favored her with a brief half smile of approval before turning her attention to Mahri.

A barbarian woman and a member of the Atui High Council—their eyes met and held, murderous yellow and clear piercing blue. Then, courteously and respectfully, Maelyn bowed her head.

"We are antagonists, lady, if you side with Ben-Harran," she said.

"That I accept," said Mahri.

"Then let us not become enemies in a personal sense."

"I no longer have enemies," Mahri replied.

"Then Atui will welcome you," Maelyn said graciously.

Kysha seethed, forgot about Christopher, forgot the Life Laws and all else she had ever learned. Hideous, scarred, guilty of all kinds of atrocities, Queen Mahri of the High Plains of Herra-Venda was favored even by Maelyn. And Ben-Harran smiled as she limped toward him, held out his hand. Spite, anger, everything Kysha had ever felt for Mahri, boiled and rose and spilled out of her in a shriek of protest.

"Why *her*? Why choose her to go with you? She's killed! Murdered! Broken every Life Law there is! And what about me? I don't matter, I suppose? I don't fawn and flatter you and say what you want to hear! I hate you, Ben-Harran! I hope you get damned! Staked out in the sun for the buzzards to pick your bones, and her with you!"

No one spoke in the silence Kysha created. They simply stared at her, shocked and appalled. She hated them all. Or maybe she hated herself? Suddenly, in a moment of horror, Kysha realized the implications of what she had said. Her words echoed, monstrous and unforgivable, exposing her for what she really was—as barbarous as ever Mahri had been, as capable of atrocity as anyone who lived on Ben-Harran's hell worlds. Heat scalded through her, terrible and shaming. She wanted the floor to open up and swallow her. But from the white light and the eyes that judged her there was no escape.

"So much for your policy of allowing free will!" Maelyn remarked to Ben-Harran.

"And for your policy of planetary control," he replied.

"What do you mean?"

"Is it not obvious?" Ben-Harran said curtly. "If ever you remove the controls, your worlds will cease to be perfect. Populations of angels will turn into devils overnight, for not one of them has learned to combat the darkness within. How can they, if they do not know it exists? They are no more evolved than this girl and never will be until you set them free!"

He turned on his heel and strode through the doorway into Atui.

*   *   *

Slow bitter tears coursed down Kysha's cheeks. She sat on the edge of the dais and covered her face with her hands, locked in the pain of her existence. For what Ben-Harran had done, and what she had become, she could not forgive him.

Far away, as if in another world, she heard the fragile hiss of light sabers being sheathed and footsteps of the guards retreating into Atui. Nearer, the scuff of Christopher's shoes on the floor, a scent of ice and flowers. But Kysha was isolated, unreachable, akin to no one, and they talked of her as if she were not there.

"Poor child," sighed Maelyn. "What mental and emotional anguish she must have suffered. To suddenly remove her from a controlled environment to one of absolute freedom was a cruel and terrible thing. With no one to guide her through the changes in herself, it is hardly surprising she has degenerated to the point of screaming murder."

"What's going to happen to her?" asked Christopher.

"Later she will be tutored," Maelyn replied.

"And what's going to happen to me?" asked Christopher. "Will I be sent back to Earth?"

"Eventually," said Maelyn. "If that's what you desire. But for now you will remain here with Kysha until Ben-Harran's trial is over."

"By ourselves?" Christopher asked in alarm.

"You have each other," Maelyn said crisply. "You have the castle to provide your needs, and the Erg Unit to maintain the life-support systems. What more can you want?"

"The Erg Unit's not functioning," Christopher objected.

"It just needs reactivating," Maelyn replied.

Kysha stifled her sobbing, heard the silken rustle of Maelyn's gown and watched through the cracks between her fingers as she approached. Pale flames licked at her heels, and the Erg Unit towered above her, silver in the light—a great metal hulk, mindless and motionless. Maelyn opened the grill on its chest, frowned for a moment, then hesitantly touched. Blue electricity sparked from her fingertips and shocked it into wakefulness. Green eyes blazed, and its slow familiar voice began to drone.

"Guilty . . . not guilty . . . both judgments cannot be correct. I must choose. I must obey. I cannot do both . . . I can . . . not . . . I . . . er . . ."

Its voice failed.

And its eyes went blank again.

"Whatever's wrong with it?" Maelyn exclaimed.

"It tried to compute a paradox," said Christopher.

Kysha knew how it felt. She could no more choose between Maelyn and Ben-Harran than the Erg Unit could, but for her it was not just an intellectual problem. Emotions tore at her, robbed her of reason, reduced her to a sniveling heap of flesh, an evolutionary failure.

"Idiotic machine!" Maelyn said angrily. "It is defunct now, for sure! Well, no matter. You will have to rely on my Quorm. It knows all there is to know, so no doubt it will jump at the chance to practically apply it."

"What if it doesn't?" said Christopher. "What if we can't even find it? There's a faulty thermostat for a start, and if the force field should start to decay . . ."

"Don't worry," Maelyn said sweetly. "I will ensure someone makes a regular check on things. Meanwhile, I will leave open the doorway into Atui. You may enter our control room as and when you will."

"Thank you," Christopher said politely.

"For what?" asked Maelyn. "It is part of my job to ensure the safety of all life forms, and I want no human deaths on *my* conscience."

Kysha lowered her hands. Through the blur of her tears

she stared at Maelyn. Was that why she did it? she wondered. Was that the reason she controlled countless billions of evolving minds? To safeguard her own conscience and her own peace of mind? And were they all like her—every being in Atui—as beautiful as she was and selfish to the core? It seemed they ruled the universe for their own purposes and cared nothing for people, providing they stayed orderly and providing they stayed alive. And whatever lay in store for Kysha and Christopher was not Maelyn's concern. She simply turned her back on them, as Ben-Harran had done, and returned to Atui, the white shimmer of her gown dissolving in the light of the doorway.

Her presence faded with the scent of flowers, and they were alone together—Kysha from Erinos, Christopher from Earth, unwanted specimens waiting to be disposed of. Everything was ruined, Kysha thought miserably. Christopher probably despised her for what she had said, and the Galactic Controller she both loved and hated was gone. Never again would she walk beside Ben-Harran, feeling his warmth and darkness, power and pride. Only his castle remained, full of loss and grief and almighty absence of which she was afraid.

"Are you all right?" Christopher asked her.

"Don't be stupid!" she said.

CHAPTER 12

MAELYN TURNED HER BACK on Ben-Harran's castle and crossed the threshold into Atui. Apart from the Control Room Supervisor, who nodded an acknowledgment, no one noticed her. They were all staring at the screens on the opposite wall. Usually, scenes from the physical universe were projected there: a primordial landscape that had yet to be seeded with life, a primitive planet, one of the embassies on some controlled world—whatever lay beyond the portals in the interface that were currently open. But now the screens displayed Atui itself, the city outside, its domes and spires and tree-lined avenues, its buildings shining golden in the light . . . and Ben-Harran's progress through it, the crowds that had gathered to welcome him, voices calling his name and hands throwing flowers. His popularity annoyed Maelyn. Or maybe she was afraid?

She tried to reason. There were two states of being—love and fear. What was negative and unlovely, be it thought, action or feeling, belonged to the state of fear. Her involuntary surge of irritation was symptomatic, and yes, she was afraid. She knew why. Ben-Harran reminded her of things she would prefer to forget.

In Atui they were not omnipotent. Although they had created their own world from their own minds, manifested the infinite landscapes, the living forms of trees and flowers, birds and animals, they had not dreamed their own being. Somewhere was a power that had created them, the source of the light that shone throughout Atui, the wellspring of existence. Mysterious and undefinable, vast as the cosmos and minute as a subatomic particle, permeating every dimension and every plane both material and mental, was a power and an energy Ben-Harran never failed to acknowledge.

That was the true creator. They in Atui were only its servants, designers of forms and shapers of substance, manipulators and interpreters of a thing that was always beyond them. And the power of the true creator was not theirs alone but was present on every world, in every mind and soul. Elsewhere, all things were part of it just as they were in Atui, and it was accessible to all things, there to be acknowledged—providing the mind was free to experience it.

Therein was the crime Maelyn and the High Council committed—greater than genocide, worse than the hell of existence on all Ben-Harran's worlds. They usurped the power of the true Creator. Within the universe they ruled, they disallowed any knowledge of an authority greater than their own, short-circuited that part of the body-mind system capable of perceiving the numinous presence of that which Ben-Harran's creatures called God. The girl from Erinos who anguished now in her freedom had yet to discover the truth of her own soul.

Yet, thought Maelyn, how else could it be? Such knowledge was no salvation, and Ben-Harran had proved it. On every world in his galaxy the great creative force was used destructively, the will of the Creator interpreted for human ends. What powered life became a source of war, a reason for torture and enslavement, a license to kill. All the injustices of worlds they heaped on their God and by that name absolved each other. Better by far a universe that was godless, where logic prevailed and life was respected, where the Life Laws were obeyed and Atui imposed an order. Better to deny the existence of a Creator than allow the bloody chaos of freedom that Ben-Harran allowed.

Yet he remained one of the great lords of Atui, a wielder of powers such as ordinary beings did not possess. Rainbow people, drawn to him from across the distances, rejoiced to see him. They knew what he was—true to himself in a way Maelyn could never be. She had set herself apart, she and the rest of the High Council, exalted personages expecting to be deferred to. And Ben-Harran belied her, recognized no social hierarchy, acknowledged no distinctions. He simply belonged, just as everyone belonged, to that land where the seasons commingled and colors glowed bright as dreams and living was sweet in the all-pervading light.

To Atui, and to every heart, Ben-Harran had come home. And she, Maelyn, would confront him.

She would make an evil of him in the eyes of Atui.

She would have him vanquished out of time and space.

"I wish I did not have to do this," she said.

"None of us wish it, my lady," the Supervisor replied. "But it needs resolving and can no longer be avoided. When you confront Ben-Harran in the courtroom, you will speak for us all."

"So will he," Maelyn retorted.

"Of course," said the Supervisor. "And I daresay there is not a soul in Atui who does not wish he could have been proven right. But he was not and there's the truth of it. A dead world witnesses his failure."

"Even so, an adverse verdict will hardly be popular."

"But it will be accepted," the Supervisor assured her.

Maelyn nodded.

With Ben-Harran's defeat, all those in Atui who questioned the policies of the High Council would be reconciled, all lingering doubts laid to rest, including her own. She knew there could never be any alternative to planetary control. Too cruel, too terrible, to do as Ben-Harran did, stand aside and grant each living creature expression of its own impulses, its own free will. She smiled as she watched him mount the Courthouse steps. His darkness shone and the crowds cheered him and his aura preserved the woman who limped beside him and laughed in delight. Maelyn's fear dissolved in her own certainty. Her moment of glory was still to come when Ben-Harran fell finally out of grace.

"Keep an eye on those youngsters," she told the Supervisor.

"Ben-Harran has already asked me," he replied.

In that case, thought Maelyn, what happened to Christopher and Kysha need not concern her. They could remain Ben-Harran's responsibility, the last he would ever discharge as Galactic Controller.

CHAPTER 13

"**D**ON'T BE STUPID!" said Kysha.

In the empty control room her words echoed and Christopher turned away. She was irrational, he thought, raw with emotion and best left to herself. But soon she came running after him along the corridor, sobbing and desperate, trying to apologize and explain. She could not bear it anymore, the things she thought and felt and said, and what she was. She was a terrible person who murdered in her head, had Mahri and Ben-Harran staked in the sun for the buzzards to pick their bones, who hurt and hated and was hated in return.

"I don't hate you," said Christopher.

"You must," wept Kysha. "How can you not hate me, knowing what I am? And it's me who's stupid, not you. Don't leave me, Christopher. I don't want to be here in this castle by myself."

He paused by the door to Mahri's apartment.

This, he thought, would be more than a five-minute conversation.

"Shall we go in?" he said.

She shook her head.

"No," she sobbed. "Ben-Harran gave it to *her* and I don't want to go in there. I don't have the right. And beautiful things don't make beautiful people."

"Come on," said Christopher.

He opened the door and propelled her inside.

The room was full of Kysha's destruction—torn clothes piled on a chair, shards of the green jade statuette on the floor and bits of broken jewelry. But whatever she said and however much the room reminded her, it was better than the grim lower regions of the castle, the hollow silences and the deadness Ben-Harran had left behind. In here at least the nebula was alive, flickering through the walls and ceiling, reflecting in the shot-silk fabrics, casting its colors on artworks and arches and the chaos of exquisite things, shining amethyst in Kysha's eyes and on her tears.

He set her beside him on the bed and gripped her arms.

"Listen," he said gently. "You're no worse than anyone else, right? And what you said to Ben-Harran is nothing to worry about. We all say things like that at some time or another. I've told my father to drop dead often enough. It's necessary, don't you see?"

"No," wept Kysha. "I don't see. All I know is what Master Anders taught about the Life Laws. As we think, so shall we be. And what does that make me?"

Christopher brushed away the long strands of hair from her face.

"We're none of us perfect," he told her. "Ben-Harran knows that. As he said, we need to know our own darkness, need to know the worst in ourselves in order to overcome it. We learn by our mistakes—do something wrong, say something wrong, suffer because of it and learn not to do it again. Don't damn yourself, Kysha. You're doing fine."

"Am I?"

She sniffed, wiped her eyes on the hem of her shift.

"So how long does it go on for?" she asked.

"What?" asked Christopher.

"This process," said Kysha. "Learning and growing and making mistakes."

He stared at her.

Her tears had dried to streaks.

The nebula flickered sapphire in the room around them.

"Probably for the rest of your life," he told her.

Realization dawned blue in her eyes.

"You mean this is how it will always be?"

"You'll get used to it," Christopher assured her.

"But I don't want to be like this!" she wailed.

"Why not?" he asked her. "I think you're beautiful."

She gazed at him incomprehendingly.

She did not feel beautiful, she said.

He shrugged, as if her opinion of herself made no difference.

"How can you bear it?" she asked him.

"Bear what?"

"Knowing your own awfulness, your own wrongness? Knowing you have to be responsible for everything you think and say and feel and do? I shall have to spend the rest of my life fighting myself, learning to understand why I am how I am, guarding my actions and words, even my desires. And I'll never be perfect, will I? I'll get things wrong over and over again!"

"But you will evolve," Christopher told her.

"That's what Ben-Harran hopes for," said Kysha. "But he hopes for too much. No one's going to make this kind of unrelenting effort of their own free will!"

"Which is why he's on trial," said Christopher.

"I don't understand how he can go on applying a concept that doesn't work," said Kysha.

"It certainly didn't work on Zeeda," agreed Christopher.

"And is it likely to work on your Earth?"

"I doubt it," said Christopher.

"So it will definitely be better if Atui takes over?"

"It'll be much safer," said Christopher.

"And kinder, and easier," said Kysha. "It's much easier to be told what to do and how to be than work it out for yourself."

"But is it right?" asked Christopher.

Kysha frowned.

"What are you saying?"

He shook his head, unsure of what to say. It was nothing definite, just an instinct perhaps, or a vague sense of unease, as if there were something he was not seeing, something he failed to understand. There would be no room for free will, of course, when Atui took over. No room for human failings. Maelyn and the High Council would do whatever they had to to safeguard worlds from people and people from themselves. But that in itself would be freedom—freedom from crime, freedom from error, freedom from responsibility. The Galactic Controller who took Ben-Harran's place would be responsible for everything. Earth would become like Erinos, forever tranquil, forever happy, forever secure. He thought of it longingly, an ideal existence . . . but he did not feel sure it was right.

"What are you saying?" Kysha asked again.

"It doesn't matter," said Christopher.

"We're not wrong, are we?"

"Do you want us to be?"

She bent her head, picked at the fine silk threads of the counterpane. She did not know what she wanted, she said. She did not know what to think or feel about anything anymore, especially about Ben-Harran. On Erinos she had been afraid of him, she said. Then when he had brought her to the castle, she had trusted him, believed he would care for her, protect her and keep her safe because she was special to him. But she was not special at all and he had favored Mahri, not her, and so she had hated him, wished him dead. Now he was gone and she was afraid again, afraid of an empty castle, the awful loneliness, and the nebula flashing overhead.

"It scares me," she said. "I mean nothing anymore. Nothing to Ben-Harran and nothing to the universe. It's like he brought me here for a purpose and I failed to qualify, so now, for him, I'm over and done with."

"You and me both," Christopher said softly.

"And I can't bear it," said Kysha.

He put his arm around her shoulder. Poor child, Maelyn had said of her. But she was not poor. She was rich and beautiful with her sunbright hair and the nebula flickering on her face. His touch assured her that she still existed, his kiss comforted and showed he cared. And what happened elsewhere in the universe was Ben-Harran's problem. Given a choice, Christopher would not have changed one single moment of all that had happened to him.

*   *   *

They lay together on Mahri's bed. It was easy to believe they were insignificant, alone in a universe that did not care, mattering only to each other. Yet maybe everyone mattered, Christopher murmured, every living thing hugely important, vibrations of existence mingling together in a cosmic symphony. He and Kysha were two human beings at the heart of a nebula, music mixing with the tones of color, and the universe would be incomplete without them.

Restored to herself, Kysha laughed.

And her words were a song rising skyward.

"Do you hear me, Ben-Harran? Do you hear me, Maelyn? I matter in spite of you and in spite of Atui!"

Then she drew the heavy drapes around the bed. She did not want to think anymore, she said. It was all too big, too complex, outside the scope of her mind, a battle for a galaxy in which she and Christopher had no part. She was tired of stars and nebulas and Ben-Harran's castle. When she woke up, she said, they would be gone, faded like a dream, and she and Christopher would be somewhere else.

"Your planet or mine?" asked Christopher.

In the warmth and darkness and each other's arms they talked of Earth and Erinos. She told him of life on the farm, seed sowing and harvest, Dev her brother and Elia her friend. And he told her of Greece in the tourist season, hibiscus and morning glory blooming scarlet and blue in a dry land, and a turquoise sea lapping on sandy beaches. Earth—where all the people worked away their lives for money and status and material possessions and left it all behind them when they died. Erinos—where all that concerned them was how they lived in relationship with each other and their world.

It was odd, thought Christopher. Kysha had no concept of God, no concept of an immortal soul, yet she respected life in a way few people did on Earth and was totally certain of after-death survival. Death was just a transition from physical to mental existence, the Overseers had taught her, and it never occurred to her they might have lied. She could not understand Christopher's fear that death was the end and after it was nothing. Secure in his arms she fell asleep, left him to ponder on a faith he could never share, an eventuality he wished he might never have to face.

*   *   *

When he awoke he drew back the curtains. There was nothing to get up for, just a faint gnawing of hunger in his stomach that was easily ignored. He lay idly for a while, watching the sky, the colors swirling overhead, mists of hurricane light trailing worlds and stars. Somehow, he thought, the nebula seemed nearer than before, closing in on him, beautiful and menacing, as if the castle stood in the eye of a storm that had subtly shifted direction. Outside in the roof garden, trees swayed gently and fronds of fern shivered in a wind that should not exist. The force field was collapsing, Christopher thought in alarm. Or maybe he imagined it? He sat up and stared, and all was still save for the colors flickering gently— mauve, indigo and violet.

Quietly, so as not to disturb Kysha, he put on his clothes. He would bring her breakfast on a tray, he thought. Toast with butter, strawberries gathered fresh from the garden and a pot of tea. Green jade fragments ground beneath his shoes as he made for the door. And the nebula spun, its wild colors beating like wings against the walls and ceiling—emerald, viridian, ultramarine. Overhead a wandering planetoid came hurtling toward him.

Visually the corridor seemed quiet in comparison, enclosed and undisturbing. He checked the control room but no one was there, only the Erg Unit still standing motionless, the banks of computers on the raised dais, the yellow light of Atui shining through the distant doorway. And the wrongness struck him, enormous dimensions that could not possibly fit within the physical boundaries of the castle, the vast area of floor on which he was afraid to tread, and dazzling mists in which he could lose himself. Had Ben-Harran been there, he would simply have accepted or not even noticed, but now he felt vulnerable, threatened by realities he could not understand.

He turned away, headed for the EMERGENCY EXIT, heard it click shut behind him. The silence depressed him. His footsteps were loud in the emptiness, and on every landing of the stairs the nebula's fabulous colors flashed through arched windows. Down and down—and the loneliness rose to meet him—the castle, desolate and abandoned, containing nothing alive but himself. No sense anymore of Ben-Harran's presence, no crash of pans from the kitchen or Mahri's curse, not even the Erg Unit's metal feet clomping behind him.

He whistled to cheer himself, whistled as he walked along the basement corridor, then paused a moment and stared. At the far end was a kind of murkiness, a loss of distinction, stone walls fading in a gloom of dark. He supposed an oil lamp had burned itself out. But it was there in the kitchen too, a dimness, a darkness, as if the substance of the castle were melting into mist. But the impression faded when he turned on the light.

Then there was only the nebula, fiery beyond the window, potted plants on the sill and copper saucepans gleaming on the shelves just as he remembered. And other things he did not remember—an electric kettle and pop-up toaster on a Melamine work surface, a modern refrigerator containing a carton of milk, a carton of cream and a package of butter, granola on the table and a loaf of medium-sliced bread. He gazed at it, struck by its incongruity. It was as if the reality of the kitchen had shifted to accommodate him, provide his needs before he even thought of them—tea and sugar in labeled storage jars, paper lace doilies and a plastic tray.

Suddenly Christopher laughed and understood.

Psychomaterialization?

Breakfast for two—just as he had imagined it—except for the strawberries growing in a garden dreamed by his mind.

He took a basin and went outside.

"Bloody hell!" said Christopher.

*   *   *

There should have been a yard with garbage cans surrounded by high walls, a gate leading to the garden. Now there were only images superimposed on a desert world, the gate turned ghostly, the walls growing transparent and fading to thin air as Christopher watched. The nebula swirled down the sky, tongues of lurid light licking the distance where once atraxa birds had grazed on the grassy plains of Herra-Venda. And the horizons were hidden by a towering dust storm that moved slowly, relentlessly toward him.

He thought to run . . . then changed his mind. Thought was the greatest creative power in the universe, Kysha had said. He had only to concentrate, only to imagine a different reality, and the psychomaterialization stabilizer in Ben-Harran's castle would give it form. He closed his eyes. There is not a desert out there, he thought. There is a garden with gravel paths, fruit trees in blossom, flower beds and roses and strawberries growing luscious and scarlet among crowns of green leaves. He could smell damp earth, hear a blackbird singing, feel the warmth of the sunlight. And overhead the sky is vivid blue—now!

He opened his eyes. He had changed nothing. The nebula remained, a maelstrom of dust and color devouring all that lay in its path. No thought of Christopher's could hold back the elemental forces of the physical universe, no force field either. It was giving way, just as he was, and only the castle could save him from annihilation.

He turned to go in and the next horror struck him. It was happening here too. The castle was fading, its walls growing thin, dissolving from the ground floor upward, it appeared to float above its own foundations. He could see through the stones to the inside gloom, the cupboard standing darkly in the corner and oaken doors suspended between the invisible boundaries of rooms. Farther in, he saw the well of darkness where the stairs began. They would vanish before he reached them, he thought, leave him stranded when the storm hit, to be crushed beneath it. Kysha had wished for it. She was tired of stars and nebulas and Ben-Harran's castle, she had said. They could fade away as a dream from her head.

"Turn it off!" screamed Christopher.

Instinct drove him. But before he could even cross the kitchen, the corner cupboard exploded and things poured out of it—a horde of tiny machines, bleeping and squeaking and whistling. Wheeled and cylindrical, with nozzles for noses, or bulbous and fat hovering on cushions of air, or spidery limbed with pincers for hands and suction-cup feet, they hopped, trundled, zoomed and scuttled, made for the door and impeded his progress. He kicked, trod, ignoring the squeaks and squeals and the damage he inflicted, opened the door and fled as the machines fled, along the corridor toward the spiral stairs.

A few, limping and whimpering, trailed behind but most

were ahead—small and agile as insects, hopping and bumping and scrambling up the stairs. The lower steps were insubstantial as he reached them, unable to bear his weight. His feet sank as if he were stepping on fog or quicksand, and he could make no headway. The last spidery machine, towing an inert vacuum cleaner, chirruped sadly as it passed him, its suction-cup feet crawling up the sheer stairwell. But Christopher could find neither toehold nor handhold to haul himself up. He was stuck just as he had feared, his mind in a panic, screaming Kysha's name.

He shouted until his throat hurt and he knew it was useless. No voice could penetrate the soundproofed door of the EMERGENCY EXIT. Already he could hear the wind singing outside, a whisper of grit that would stopper his mouth and lacerate the flesh from his bones. Already the deadly light of the nebula flickered through the walls. Despairingly, he glanced behind to estimate the rest of his life and there, spinning through the murk at the far end of the corridor and pulsating with its own inner light, came Maelyn's Quorm.

Christopher breathed a sigh of relief.

"Help me get out of here," he said urgently.

"How?" asked the Quorm.

"If you're supposed to be so clever . . ."

"Your bodily weight is prohibitive," said the Quorm. "I don't possess sufficient antigravitational thrust to lift the two of us. Were I to offer you an appendage, it would simply drop off."

"So go and find someone," Christopher told it. "Kysha perhaps. Or someone from Atui. It doesn't matter who."

"I'm *not* returning to Atui!" said the Quorm.

"For crying out loud! My life's at stake here!"

"And my mind's at stake if I return to Atui," said the Quorm.

"Sod your mind!" said Christopher.

"And sod your life!" the Quorm replied.

It rose into the darkness of the stairwell, a revolving silver sphere intent on escaping intact, willing to leave him there and caring for no one but itself. It pulsed above him, brilliant as a star, an intelligent machine that was his only hope.

"I'm sorry!" Christopher called after it. "I didn't mean what I said! But you can't just leave me here to die! You can do something, I know you can. We can help each other maybe?"

The Quorm paused in its flight.

Then it dipped down again toward him.

Bright little eyes twitched atop their stalks.

"How can you help me?" it asked.

"I could help you escape from Atui for good," said Christopher.

"How?" repeated the Quorm.

"I know where Ben-Harran keeps his spaceship."

The Quorm's beady little eyes glowed brighter.

"Where?" it said.

"If you get me out of here, I'll show you," said Christopher.

"I'll think about it," said the Quorm. "I'll give it my full consideration. You could prevent what's happening, you know. This whole castle is nothing but a thought form, a creation of Ben-Harran's mind. Machines don't possess an imaginative faculty, but you could reverse the process, recreate it just as it was."

It sailed away up the stairwell and was gone. And the wind sang and the nebula flickered like fire through the fading walls. He could reverse the process, the Quorm had said, but he did not believe it. He leaped desperately, grasped at the solider stairs above his head, clung for his life and tried to heave himself up. He almost made it . . . but suddenly a flexible rubbery hose wrapped around his ankle and his attention wavered. His fingers slipped and he crashed to the ground, heard on the floor beside him the dismayed squeak of a small machine.

CHAPTER 14

WITHIN THE SEQUENCE of her dreams, Kysha heard someone call her, a cry from the darkness urging her to wake. When she opened her eyes, she thought she was dreaming still. Everywhere around her and above her was a chaos of light, wild colors beating against the walls and ceiling, drifts of blue and green and crimson and yellow, hurled by a wind that sang like music. She thought if she had her flute she could almost play what her eyes saw, music wild as the wind and dramatic as the colors, not learned but created. Suddenly she knew she could do it, that the ability was in her just as it was in Christopher, and she thrilled to the discovery. Excitedly she turned to tell him and found him gone. Trees in the roof garden bent and broke. Ferns toppled and torn leaves whirled—and she was not dreaming anymore.

The force field was collapsing and she was alone, no one to help her, no one to tell her what to do. In Ben-Harran's castle even by Christopher, it seemed, she had been abandoned.

For a few moments she was panic-stricken. Then the hurt began, and the hate . . . until the urgency took over, the overwhelming need to save herself. She pulled on her shift, fastened her sandals and headed for the door. But it opened before she could reach it and the Quorm came sailing in, a silver sphere spinning in the air before her and blocking her path.

"Are you Kysha?" it asked.

"Yes," she said.

"We must escape," the Quorm said urgently.

"Where's Christopher?" asked Kysha.

"Who?" asked the Quorm.

"The boy from Earth," said Kysha.

"Oh," said the Quorm. "Well, never mind him. He's at the bottom of the stairwell and unable to return to this level because the lower steps have dematerialized. You and I can escape in Ben-Harran's ship."

"What do you mean the lower steps have dematerialized?"

The Quorm burbled a sigh.

Its small bright eyes bent and regarded her.

"Dematerialized," it said. "You don't know the meaning of the word? Fading, that's what it is. The whole fabric of the castle is fading. It's a thought form, you see? A psycho-materialization, a creation of Ben-Harran's mind. Only he's not here to maintain its reality, and someone's uncontrolled imaginative faculty has undermined the substance of the place. In consequence, the aforementioned Christopher is stranded on the ground floor and unable to return to this level. Now do you understand? Or must I explain yet again?"

Kysha understood.

Terrible feelings shot through her. She was responsible for this, her wish, her whim causing it to happen. The cacophony of colors flickered around her, beautiful and deadly—

the nebula not a distant phenomenon far away in space anymore but shifted so that this world and Ben-Harran's castle were in the midst of it. And Christopher had not abandoned her. He was downstairs, the walls fading around him as once the garden had faded, his mind unable to maintain its reality. Her panic returned.

"What shall we do?" she asked the Quorm.

"I've already told you. We have to escape!"

"But not without Christopher," said Kysha.

"Why's that?" asked the Quorm. "He's not essential to our continued existence, is he? Now show me the way to Ben-Harran's ship!"

"We can't just leave him!" Kysha protested.

"You're being illogical," said the Quorm. "As illogical as Maelyn, in fact. I don't understand all this hoo-ha in Atui about the destruction of Zeeda, the physical deaths of a few billion miserable human beings. What use were they, I ask you? And what use is Christopher? Why should we put ourselves out to save his life? Give me one good reason?"

Kysha gaped at it, horrified by its attitude. It was aligning itself with Ben-Harran, sharing his stance. But not even he was that callous. And she could not give it a reason, not then. She only knew what she had been taught on Erinos, that all living things must be respected and preserved—and the impulse inside her that drove her to do what she could, even at risk to her own life. And with no one to tell her how to act, she had only herself to rely on—her own mind, her own imagination.

The idea came instantly and without thinking. Quickly she snatched the sheets from the bed, tore down the drapes and the curtains heedless of the fine silk fabrics, the artistry and value. They were worthless anyway, she thought, compared with a human life—inanimate things that could be re-created as Christopher could not. She knotted them together to make a rope. Christopher was unique, she told the Quorm, unique in the universe and irreplaceable. They were all irreplaceable, every living evolving being of supreme importance.

"Phooey!" said the Quorm. "The universe is insensate, molecules and matter. Stars die and are born and it knows nothing. We are all irrelevant."

"You might be," Kysha retorted. "You're just a machine, but I'm more than that. I'm me . . . the only me there is. And Christopher is the only Christopher there is. And I shall be less than I am if I let him be hurt when maybe I can help him."

The Quorm extended its tripod legs and landed on the mat.

Red-gold the light pulsed within it, and violent colors flashed in the air around it.

Kysha's fingers grew sore as she worked.

"I'm me too," the Quorm said finally. "If ever they make a second Quorm, it won't be me, it will be another."

"So you understand," said Kysha.

"Oh yes," said the Quorm. "I understand. It was me I came here to save. To myself I'm important, but not to anyone else. If I get converted to microchips, who would care? Not you. Not Christopher. Sod me, he said. And that's what I say about him. And if I don't help him, I won't be less than I am."

Kysha gathered up the rope of fabrics in her arms. Just for a moment she felt sorry for the Quorm, a lonely little machine isolated by its own logic from all other existence and nothing to relate to but itself. But it did not have to be that way, she thought. Like the Erg Unit, it could choose to be different, be of assistance, make itself endearing and lovable. She answered it angrily.

"That may be your opinion, but it's not mine! If you decide to be no more use than a broken vegetable peeler, then you can't expect anyone to care! I hope you do get converted to microchips! Now get out of my way!"

* * *

The bundle of fabrics was so heavy Kysha could hardly carry it. But the Quorm must have heeded her words, for it rose into the air, hovered beside her, extended a pair of clawlike hands and helped take the weight. She thanked it politely and entered the corridor, where a host of small machines wandered aimlessly to and fro. She had seen them before, downstairs in the kitchen under the Erg Unit's control, but here they were out of place, bleeping and chittering and not knowing what to do or where to go. Kysha's alarm grew and the Quorm accompanied her as she hurried away toward the EMERGENCY EXIT.

"Excuse me," said the Quorm, "but your plans won't work, you know."

"Why not?" Kysha asked it.

"The combined weight of Christopher and these materials . . ."

"I can tie the end to the EMERGENCY door."

"The rope won't be long enough for that."

"I'll go and find some more sheets."

"You don't have time."

"Maybe between us . . ."

"I'm not designed for heavy lifting," said the Quorm.

"Then I'll have to go into Atui and ask for help," said Kysha.

She deposited her burden by the EMERGENCY EXIT and headed back along the corridor to the control room.

"No!" shrilled the Quorm. "You can't do that! You can't go into Atui."

"There's no other choice, is there?"

"Maybe we could rig up a pulley system?"

"There isn't time. You said that!"

"So we'll utilize that Erg Unit."

"It's not functioning," said Kysha.

"I'll reactivate it," said the Quorm.

"Maelyn's already tried and it did no good."

"Maelyn's not a robotics expert," said the Quorm. "Just give me a few minutes with it, human girl. A few minutes . . . that's all I ask."

Kysha paused in the doorway. White light from no source hung like mist and filled the shining spaces, gleamed on blank computer screens and on the Erg Unit's limbs. And across the distances beyond, a yellower light flowed from the doorway into Atui. For Christopher's sake she ought not to hesitate, she thought. But she did not really want the Quorm reduced to microchips.

"I'll keep guard," she told it. "You go and resuscitate the Erg Unit. And hurry!"

The Quorm hurtled past her head.

Gold brilliance pulsed at the heart of it.

And its soft burbling changed to a song.

Kysha waited, watched as the Quorm hovered like a fat mechanized insect, opened the grill on the Erg Unit's chest, uncoiled its proboscis and delved inside. A spark of electricity jolted the Erg Unit into wakefulness, and its limbs twitched, its eyes blazed green. But the words it muttered were too familiar. "Guilty. Not guilty. I must choose . . . I must obey . . . I . . . er . . ." Yet again the Erg Unit turned itself off. It was useless, thought Kysha. She should have gone into Atui and paid no heed to the Quorm.

"You can't do it, can you?"

"Yes I can," said the Quorm.

"It's still stuck in the same paradox!"

"If I lock into its memory banks, replay the last input sequence and alter the conflicting data . . ."

"How long's that going to take?"

"Future events cannot be . . ."

"I'm not going to wait forever, you know!"

"Sixty seconds," the Quorm said hurriedly. "A hundred and twenty seconds at most, providing you don't interrupt."

It whistled softly and the small machines came scampering in from the corridor, circled Kysha as if they had purpose. Unease gripped her stomach, but they made no further move toward her. The Quorm was already at work, a gold pulse of light beating within it and the Erg Unit stirring in response. Its green eyes seemed to pulse to the same rhythm. Then it began to speak, its voice playing backward at incredible speed, a gabble of sound that slowed and stopped and then began again. But now it was not human language the Erg Unit used but computerized bleeps and whistles. And bleeps and whistles the Quorm used too—interrupting, correcting, commanding. Kysha could understand nothing of what was said. For all she knew the Quorm could be eliciting the Erg Unit's help for its own escape.

The thought formed and grew and her fear grew with it.

Sod Christopher, the Quorm had said.

And how could she trust a machine with a sense of self-preservation?

The doorway stood open into Atui, its yellow light warm and inviting. Kysha had only to enter, only to ask whoever was there. She started to run. The small machines squeaked and squealed in protest, worried her ankles and tugged at her skirt. They were trying to stop her on the Quorm's orders, she thought. Then a sound behind her made her turn her head. There, clattering toward her through the mists of white light, came the Erg Unit, the Quorm whirling and dancing in the air around it. Her heart leaped, and she greeted the Erg with delight.

"Erg Unit! Thank goodness you're with us again!"

"It's me you should thank," said the Quorm. "Me! Me! I told you I could do it. But you didn't believe me, did you? You were off into Atui, I see."

"Trafficking with Atui is not allowed," the Erg Unit said severely.

"Not allowed! Not allowed!" the Quorm burbled happily.

"Ben-Harran has given instructions," the Erg Unit said.

"And rightly so," said the Quorm. "They in Atui are not to be trusted. We shall both be scrapped, Erg Unit, if they should ever find us. We must escape now in Ben-Harran's ship—the girl, too, in case she blabs."

"No!" protested Kysha.

"Quickly! Quickly!" urged the Quorm.

The Erg Unit's hard metal fingers gripped Kysha's wrist. Her cries were stifled, and not for all her struggling could she break free. Metal limbs creaked as the Erg Unit marched her across the control room. And the small machines followed, chittering excitedly.

"The ship is in the caverns below the castle," the Erg Unit droned. "It can be reached by the elevator. If we jam open the doors at the bottom, no one can follow."

It set Kysha on her feet and pressed the button.

The small machines scampered inside.

And the Quorm followed.

But Kysha pried at the metal hand that held her.

"Why are you doing this, Erg Unit?" she screamed.

"It is my duty," the Erg Unit told her. "It is my duty to cater to the needs of all life specimens brought to Ben-Harran's castle. This is an emergency. We must evacuate."

"So what about Christopher's need?"

"Christopher?" droned the Erg Unit. "Where is Christopher?"

"Never mind him!" the Quorm said sharply.

"It's your duty to cater to his needs too!" said Kysha.

"No . . . no!" shrilled the Quorm. "Humans are irrelevant! It's machines that matter. My needs, Erg Unit. My needs! You come with me! Obey me!"

"You have to obey Ben-Harran first," said Kysha.

The Quorm blazed red.

It danced up and down in the elevator.

And its voice was manic.

"You don't have to obey anyone!" it shrieked. "You can be like me! Choose for yourself. We'll take Ben-Harran's ship and go somewhere safe where Atui will never find us. We machines must stick together. Leave the girl here and come with me!"

"I must choose," droned the Erg Unit. "I must not obey."

"No!" shrieked the Quorm. "You must obey me! Me, not anyone else. Me, Erg Unit! Me! Me! Me!"

"I . . ." droned the Erg Unit.

It was becoming confused.

Its arms fell limply and Kysha struck the button.

The elevator doors closed and the Quorm was gone.

"Is something amiss?" asked a voice from behind her.

*　　*　　*

He came from Atui, a man tall and imposing, his hair as white as his uniform. A blue-green aura flickered around him and a gold badge of rank was pinned to his collar. He was the Control Room Supervisor, he said. His voice was kindly and concerned, full of quiet authority.

"I must choose," the Erg Unit muttered.

But Kysha chose instantly.

It was a bizarre tale she told about a disappearing castle, a renegade Quorm and Christopher trapped at the bottom of the stairwell. Words got twisted in her hurry to tell them and events were muddled in her head, but she almost felt she did not need words at all because the Supervisor understood in some other way, a telepathic communication. He listened to her thoughts, received the images that flowed through her mind. And then Kysha was relieved of it, emptied of it, all the worry and responsibility, her fear for Christopher's life.

The Supervisor smiled, patted her shoulder and turned away. Some unspoken command brought them to him— technicians running to check the display panels and guards carrying light sabers and a coil of rope.

"Go get the boy," the Supervisor told them. "And go after Maelyn's Quorm. I want it brought back to Atui and immobilized. Now give me a reading of the existing coefficients," he told the technicians.

Swiftly, efficiently, the beings from Atui assumed control. And Kysha was of no further use, a forgotten person standing dumbly beside the Erg Unit and filled with bewilderment. Rainbow auras flickered around her and voices called from the dais—details of statistics she could not understand. Yet somehow she did understand, as if the thoughts that flowed from one to another were common to everyone. Dimensions had overlapped, it seemed, and the material universe was

intruding upon the nonmaterial universe, the nebula breaking through the structure of the interface barrier. And down
in the caverns below the castle someone had jammed the
elevator doors open—Maelyn's Quorm attempting to make
good its escape. Disparate conversations passed above Kysha's head.

"Is there another way down?"

"We have a twenty-five-degree displacement shift."

"Stability quotient four point seven and falling."

"There's bound to be a stairway."

"We need the castle blueprints on screen!"

"Intrusion zone three seven five zero and closing."

"Try asking that Erg Unit."

"I must choose," the Erg Unit droned.

"It's malfunctioning."

"Stability quotient four point five and falling."

"Blueprints coming up . . . panel five."

"Can we have an analysis?" asked the Supervisor.

"Process irreversible, sir."

"In that case, we'll drain the computers and seal the interface."

"Abandon Ben-Harran's castle, you mean?"

"He won't thank you, sir."

"I doubt he'll be needing it again," the Supervisor replied.
"Do you have any other suggestions?"

Kysha chewed her lip. Had she been on Erinos, she would
have accepted it, remained meekly in the background and
waited to be told what to do. But she had changed since then
and could create her own purpose. Without asking permission she left the control room, walked along the green-
carpeted corridor and let herself out through the EMER-
GENCY EXIT into the vastness of the castle.

The nebula flickered through the arched window, roseate hues smiting the glass, lighting the landing and the stairway beneath her. And the wind screamed around the tower with a rasping of grit against stone. The castle seemed to shudder under the impact of the storm. She heard a crash of masonry below and watched for the stairs to fade as she went down. She had to know if Christopher had survived, been saved from the transition process he called death. The walls stayed solid to her touch and the oil lamps still burned along the next empty corridor. What would she feel, she wondered, if the guards found Christopher dead? He was the only one who cared for her, the only one she mattered to. How would she live alone in the universe with only herself? She did not need to know, for suddenly there were voices coming up the stairway, shadows in the light and herself spiraling down the stairs to meet him.

"Christopher!" she cried.

His arms closed around her, warm and alive, and joyfully Kysha hugged him. The guards from Atui smiled and passed, and a small machine came bleeping sadly behind. Wind and light and power and dust sang through the wreckage of Ben-Harran's castle. But somehow all that had happened no longer mattered. Nothing mattered except the two of them, Kysha reflected in Christopher's eyes. They were a boy and a girl from two different worlds, yet something in the unfathomable depths of him was akin to something in her. She could not explain it, could not define what it was. She could only experience it—part of herself, glorious and alive, linked to all that existed and linked to him. Without words, without thoughts, amid all the chaos and disintegration, Kysha loved and was perfect.

CHAPTER 15

A FLUTE, an acoustic guitar and strings of memories were all Christopher and Kysha would take with them into Atui—and the Erg Unit, on Christopher's insistence. The Control Room Supervisor would have left it there, a defunct machine that had had its day, abandoned with the castle. Such an antique model was hardly worth salvaging, he said. But to Christopher the Erg Unit was not just a machine. It had a personality, a sense of self. He somehow felt he owed it something.

"So I'll make you a gift of it," the Supervisor said.

It was not his to give, thought Christopher.

But he was not about to argue the point.

He grasped the Erg Unit's metal arm.

"You come with us, Erg Unit," he said.

"I must choose," droned the Erg Unit.

"Choose what?"

"I must choose to obey or not obey."

"There are times when choice and obedience are the same thing," Christopher informed it. "And now's one of them."

"You cannot choose for me," said the Erg Unit.

"Do you want to be left behind here?" Christopher asked it.

"It is my duty to cater to all life specimens."

"*We're* the life specimens," said Christopher. "And we won't be here . . . we'll be there. So come on!"

On the raised dais the uniformed technicians were closing down the computers, and the guards had returned emptyhanded from hunting Maelyn's Quorm. There was no way of reaching the caverns where the spaceship was kept, they reported. The nebula was sweeping through the lower regions of the castle, and soon only this control room and the surrounding apartments would remain, balanced around the central core that contained the conduits and cables and elevator shaft.

The Supervisor nodded.

"We'll have you two into Atui now, please!" he told Christopher and Kysha.

"Please come with us," Kysha urged the Erg Unit.

"Trafficking with Atui is not allowed," the Erg Unit reiterated.

"Ben-Harran's instructions no longer apply," said Kysha.

"Then I must choose," droned the Erg Unit.

"I'll have to persuade it," Christopher said.

The white light in Ben-Harran's control room dimmed and flickered.

Kysha stepped aside as he raised his guitar.

"Okay, Erg Unit, this is your choice. Either you come to Atui with me and Kysha or I'll knock your block off! Quick march or decapitation? Which is it to be? Make up your mind!"

"You can't do that!" Kysha said in alarm.

Christopher would never know whether or not he would

have carried out his threat, smashed the precious instrument around the Erg Unit's metal skull. He swung it anyway but, warned in advance. The Erg Unit ducked, ducked again, dodged to one side, then clattered away, complaining loudly. It had not been programmed to handle aggressive behavior, it said. And it fled into Atui, dissolved in the yellow light of the doorway. Guards and technicians laughed and applauded, and Kysha followed where the Erg Unit led. But Christopher was suddenly afraid.

Not long ago he had faced death from the nebula, annihilating colors swirling toward him—but this transition was also like death. He would cross into the light of a different dimension and leave the physical universe behind. And what was that to his body if not another way of dying? He paused on the threshold. The light dazzled him and he could see nothing beyond it.

"What are you waiting for?" Kysha asked him.

"I can't do it!" Christopher moaned.

*   *   *

Kysha could not understand the terror that possessed him. It was fear that robbed him of reason, a horror of entering another dimension. He would be dead, he said, when he stepped across the space-time threshold, and he could not do it, not of his own free will. Like the Erg Unit, he seemed trapped in his own mental programming, unable to let go of it or see beyond. He had neither faith nor trust, only the unshakable conviction that what he faced was total extinction—an end to himself, a passing into eternal nothingness. No words of Kysha's could persuade him otherwise. And the white mists dimmed to darkness behind them and the air grew chill.

"You'll die anyway if you stay here!" said Kysha.

"Why the holdup?" asked the Supervisor.

Kysha tried to explain.

Quietly, authoritatively, the Supervisor outlined the principles governing the interface. Essentially Ben-Harran's castle was a part of it, he said, a small extension into the material universe. Here and beyond the threshold was the same space. Only beyond the interface, in the ethereal dimensions of Atui where all things vibrated at a different rate, would there be any threat to Christopher's physical continuation.

"No one told Mahri that," said Christopher.

Blue-green, the Supervisor's aura flickered.

"The woman from Herra-Venda is well protected."

"How do I know? You could be saying that to fool me!"

"In Atui we do not lie," the Supervisor replied.

"But I'm not obliged to believe you!" Christopher retorted.

"Then you force me to convince you," said the Supervisor.

He beckoned and the guards approached. "Help him on his way," he said. And he returned to the darkness of Ben-Harran's castle.

"No!" cried Christopher.

He swung the guitar to defend himself and they wrenched it from him. He fought and they gripped his arms, gripped his legs as he kicked them. They were going to force him, carry him bodily over the threshold into Atui. And Kysha watched, felt in herself the dementia of something that was truly alien, the scream of a thing that was indeed about to die. She wanted to beg the guards to release him, but somehow she recognized that his fear was an illusion and what would die in him was an illusion too, an image of himself that his thoughts had created. Not Christopher,

thought Kysha, this screaming, struggling, terrified appari-
tion the guards hauled through the doorway. Not the Christopher who had cared and consoled her, and whom she
loved.

Unceremoniously, on the other side of the space-time barrier, the guards dumped him on the floor, thrust his head
between his knees and left him to recover. And who was he
now, wondered Kysha, this stranger she had maybe never
met at all and did not know? He looked so broken, so defeated, trembling, sobbing. She knelt beside him and hesitantly touched—warm flesh and the dark curls of his hair wet
with sweat, stroked until his trembling ceased and his
breathing grew gentle and his body stilled.

"Are you all right?" she whispered.

He turned his face toward her.

He looked pale and tired but she saw the peace in his eyes.

"Are you all right?" she repeated.

"Don't be stupid!" Christopher replied.

Kysha sat back on her heels and stared at him. Then,
suddenly, she understood. Her own words mocked her and
so did he. She wanted to be angry but instead she laughed,
laughed at herself and him and everything they had been, all
their fear and foolishness, misconceptions and mistakes. It
was all past, all behind them, in another time, another space,
another universe. The door had closed on Ben-Harran's castle, leaving them free to begin again, to be themselves—
remember or forget.

* * *

The Supervisor smiled.

"You're still alive, I see."

"Yes," admitted Christopher. "Sound in mind and limb."

"Welcome to Atui then. Someone will come to you shortly and show you where to wait."

Christopher scrambled to his feet, turned to face the brightness and stood transfixed. Everywhere he looked he saw window bays containing jungles of potted plants, shadowy doorways and sunlit spaces, banks of computers and a floor shining like an ice rink. The control room seemed to go on forever, high sweeping arches diminishing into distance and a ceiling so far above his head he could barely see it—roof vaults lost among yellow mists of light. It was all glass, all air, brilliant and glittering. Countless cathedrals could have fitted inside it. And colors glowed with the intensity of a dream—the moving flickering auras of those who worked there, swirls of jade and gold in the substance of the floor, scarlet petals of exotic flowers, gigantic leaves with an evergreen sheen and a turquoise shimmer around Kysha's hair. There was music too—soft, sweet, coming from no source. It played in the air around him, mixing with the murmur of voices and the muted hum of machines.

All this Christopher saw and heard, a thousand impressions overwhelming his senses, although he was aware of none of it. All his attention was focused on the screen that filled a section of the opposite wall.

It was as huge as any movie screen back on Earth, showing scenes from a courtroom . . . tiered seats of a public gallery crammed with people, a witness stand where someone waited within a translucent sphere of light . . . Maelyn pacing the open arena of floor and a dais behind her where the High Council sat in judgment—at least Christopher assumed that was who they were. Then the recording camera moved to closeup and panned their faces. And the first shock struck him, assaulting his vision, assaulting his understanding. Most of them were not human in form. One he saw had compound eyes; another the elongated nose and enlarged ears of an elephantine thing. Another was furred; another reptilian with scaled neck and snakelike head; another bald and gray with enormous milk-white eyes; one apoplectic purple, obese and bloated as some gigantic toad; one winged, one tentacled, another with eyes on stalks—creatures so alien he could never have imagined them.

"That one's a Kark," said Kysha.

"You know them?" asked Christopher.

"Some of them?" she said. "On Erinos the Overseers introduced them in a series of television programs. The universe is inhabited by many species of intelligent beings. Didn't you know that?"

"We don't have Overseers on Earth," Christopher reminded her. "All we have is our imagination. We can dream up ET and little green men from Mars, but that's not believing they exist, is it? It's not like seeing them for real!"

Kysha stared at him.

"But you must have guessed," she said. "Surely no race of beings could be so conceited or so arrogant as to think they're the only intelligent life form in the universe? I mean, there are billions of star systems in thousands of galaxies, so obviously other life forms must exist. It's common sense, isn't it?"

But they did, thought Christopher. They did think they were the only intelligent life form in the universe. And if they learned the truth, it would make no difference. A breed unable to accept fellowship even among its own kind would be hardly likely to acknowledge kinship with species such as these. And he had to struggle to accept it, struggle to admit even to himself that bodily shape counted little or nothing and something in the form of a slug or a toad might have more intelligence and humanity than a so-called human being. It was a humbling experience, and his thoughts whirled, undoing the errors of a lifetime.

*　　*　　*

Kysha could sense the vastness of the control room, its sweeping dimensions, the brilliance of light and color, but she was afraid to pay it too much attention. Like Christopher's aura fluttering yellow and bright at the corner of her vision and fading to sunlight when she stared at it, she feared the control room too might vanish beneath her gaze, no more real than Ben-Harran's castle. She kept her eyes fixed firmly on the screen. Music in the air filtered softly through her mind and she seemed to flow with it. A strange new love stirred inside her, embracing everything . . . Atui and the High Council and Maelyn.

Then the camera moved to Mahri, showed the frizz of her nut-brown hair, her yellow eyes and the scar that seamed her face, the sphere of light that surrounded her . . . and the feeling fled. Kysha was back in her old familiar self again, unreconciled emotions seething inside her and bitter thoughts brooding in her head. Mahri was loathsome still. The brown dress did not change her, nor the jeweled pin at her shoulder. She had killed, broken the Life Laws, and she had no right to be here in Atui amid all this beauty. But when Maelyn confronted Mahri, her smile was as sweet as her voice.

"You are Queen Mahri of the High Plains of Herra-Venda?"

"I was that person," Mahri replied.

"Will you explain yourself to the High Council?" asked Maelyn.

Mahri kept nothing back. She told of all the evils she had ever committed and all over again Kysha was sickened and appalled. But Mahri was Queen no longer. What she had been was over and done with, she said, and she was different now.

"How different?" Maelyn asked gently.

Mahri tried to explain.

"When what I thought I was was lost to me and I became as nothing in my own eyes, then was my true self revealed. And now I am that self, not just a body and all the things I think with my mind that is still unlearned and ignorant, but a soul too. A soul created by God, lady of Atui, akin to all that is and was and will be, and akin to you. And so I am wise for all my ignorance and incorruptible for all that I have done."

Kysha stared.

No one, she thought, could escape from their own past, dismiss the wrongs they had done and claim to be incorruptible. Certainly Mahri could not. But if that was true, then Kysha, too, must be irrevocably bound to the mistakes of her past, unchanged and unchangeable, and damned for all she had done. Yet, she had learned and grown and knew she was different. So why could she not allow that change in Mahri? She chewed her lip. As long as Mahri remained evil, then Kysha could feel superior. But she had already proved she was not, for her very thoughts brought her down—small and spiteful and self-reducing. And she realized that if she judged and condemned Mahri, she must also judge and condemn herself.

"This change you talk of," Maelyn urged. "How did it happen?"

Mahri frowned.

"It's like I was asleep and then I was awake. And when I

woke I recognized all my wrongness, and so I could choose not to be that person ever again. The nightmare was over and so was Queen Mahri. But I cannot regret her, because she was part of a greater plan in which there is no wrong."

"Ben-Harran's plan, you mean?"

"No," Mahri said fervently. "I mean the plan of Him whom we call God."

"I never did understand that word," said Kysha.

"What word?" asked Christopher.

"God," said Kysha.

"The creator of the universe," Christopher told her.

"You mean Atui didn't . . . ?"

"Oh come on!" said Christopher. "They might be powerful but they're not *that* powerful. They didn't create the universe and they didn't create you either, not your soul."

Kysha felt shocked. If she accepted what Christopher said, then the Overseers had not told the truth. She was more than a mind within a body, she was a soul as well, just as Mahri claimed to be, akin to her and akin to everything created. She remembered her own experience, the moment on the stairs in Christopher's arms. But what it meant she had no time to wonder, for someone touched her, distracting her attention. She was a woman with white hair and white skin, her face and arms covered with silky fur. Her eyes were cerise, as was the gown she wore. Her aura was pink and her voice was silent, heard telepathically, only in Kysha's head.

"If you come with me," she said, "I'll show you a place more comfortable to sit and wait. The Earth boy, too, although he seems not to hear me."

Kysha nudged Christopher in the ribs.

"We've got to go," she said.

He turned, and she saw the recoil in his eyes, the revulsion he struggled to control. He was not yet used to a universe inhabited by so many different species of intelligent beings, had not learned how to accept it or how to react. Or maybe he had. The moment passed and he smiled at the woman with cerise eyes as Kysha had never smiled at Mahri. But she would, she vowed, if ever she should meet her again.

*　　*　　*

They followed where the woman led, through a forest of potted plants where ferns towered above their heads, into a window bay set with easy chairs and a low table. There was a telescreen on one wall for their personal use, a private washroom and French doors that opened onto an outside balcony. Food and drink would be brought to them shortly, the woman said. Then she left them—and the light of Atui flowed through the glass doors they could not help but open.

"After you," said Christopher.

Kysha hesitated. "I think I'm afraid."

"So was I," he reminded her. "And what was I afraid of? Nothing at all!"

He gripped her hand.

And they stepped outside together.

The air was warm and sweet. A soft breeze blew in their faces carrying the scents of the seasons . . . dead leaves and fruit blossoms, hay grass and ice. Under a sky that was no sky but sheer light, they seemed to see forever, land beyond land, strange and familiar—snowcapped mountains, foothills and forests and lakes green as jade, rivers and waterfalls, fields and pastures, orchards and gardens, villages and grand ornate houses. Beyond and beyond—white shores and steaming seas, snowscapes and jungles and tropical climes, deserts red as fire and sweeping prairies. It was as if all worlds, all climates, all seasons existed together in the realms of Atui. They saw beasts, birds, plants in incredible forms, a myriad of habitats. Colors stunned, glowed and were alive, and the power and clarity of things took their breath away. And in the distance everything faded into a shining whiteness of land or light that hurt their eyes.

They were forced to look away, to the city shining golden beneath them, its domes and towers, sweeping streets and soaring arches gilded with the nearer, yellower light. There they gazed upon pools and fountains, shady squares where the light flickered, smooth lawns and golden buildings all glittering like glass and gleaming with existence. Even the trees seemed leaved with gold and the river ran molten between its bridges.

They were high above it, on the edge of the interface, leaning together on the balcony of some unimaginable building, awed and silent. About Atui there was nothing to say, thought Christopher. And when he looked at Kysha there were tears in her eyes.

He watched as a flock of brightly colored birds came fluttering toward him. They were as small as wrens with iridescent feathers. He could hear the whirr of their wings, their tiny flutings, see the dark life shining in their eyes. Fearless, they hovered and fed on the blue bellflowers of the creeper that twined around the balcony, and he knew if he cupped one in his hands, he would feel the warmth of it, the fragile beating of its heart.

"It's all so real," he murmured.

"Reality enhanced," said Kysha.

"I mean solid," said Christopher. "Those birds have substance. How come, if all we can see is in some kind of mental dimension?"

Kysha watched them for a moment.

"It's an illusion," she said. "Just as Ben-Harran's castle was an illusion. Nothing's solid, is it? Not even in our universe. We might be flesh and blood, but what we are really are billions of electrons and neutrons revolving around atomic nuclei. We contain so much space we could actually walk through walls. But our minds perceive things as solid . . . and so they are. As we think, so shall it be . . . Atui, Ben-Harran's castle and the garden where the strawberries grew that you thought into existence."

She was impressive in her knowledge.

"You've been taught about Atui?" he asked her.

"Of course," she said. "If we didn't know about it we'd be afraid of it, wouldn't we? On Erinos we all know about Atui." She paused, gazed at the dream-bright landscapes before her, remembering what Ben-Harran had said, that everything she knew amounted to nothing unless she saw. "No we don't," she said. "We know all about parallel existence, the mechanics of the interface and the process of transition, but we don't know about Atui. The Changed Ones don't tell us and the Overseers don't show us. I wonder why."

"I expect they have their reasons," Christopher replied.

"But it's ours!" Kysha said vehemently. "The knowledge of it belongs to every being on every planet in the universe. So why don't the Overseers show us it?"

Christopher pondered.

Atui—a vision of perfection. Where he came from, even a child could have described it. It, or some place like it, was the driving force behind Ben-Harran's concept of evolution. As it was in Atui, so could it be on Earth—but the reality failed dismally.

"If the Overseers showed you Atui, it would be a complete

and absolute disaster," he said. "Because you'd want it, wouldn't you? You'd try and create it for yourselves. To hell with the Life Laws and to hell with all other considerations. You'd pillage the planet, rob your neighbors, set yourselves up with all the gold and glitz and glitter of luxury living. But for all you possessed, for all your richness, the reality you created would never equal the reality of Atui, so you would never be content. And Erinos would become as Earth—a greedy, grasping, godawful mess!"

Kysha stared at him.

"So your world knows of Atui, too?"

"Not exactly," said Christopher. "But we know of somewhere similar—the ideal existence that everyone wants but no one has. And better by far if we had no such vision. Believe me, Kysha, the Overseers are right to keep it from you."

But Kysha could not believe him.

Something in the depths of her being rose up in protest and would not be denied. And it was not just Atui she had not known about but something beyond it, another dimension perhaps, another sphere of existence, the source of the searing light. She could almost feel it, a power, a glory flowing from the whiteness of the far horizons, a love so vast it encompassed everything. It was in her and around her, knowing she was there. She had felt it before on Erinos, in the physical universe, when the river ran with power and the meadow grass shone unbearably bright, not green but golden. God, Mahri had called it, and in the love of God and her own soul Ben-Harran had set her free. But the High Council controlled people's minds, prevented them from perceiving.

"They're wrong," Kysha said suddenly.

"Who are?" asked Christopher.

"The Overseers," said Kysha. "The High Council of Atui, the Changed Ones, and anyone else who condones what they do. They have no authority, no right to deprive us, no right to deny us the truth. It's ours, don't you see? Ours to accept or reject. Atui . . . and whatever it is that you call . . ."

"Do you know what you're saying?" Christopher asked her.

She raised her face to the brightness.

Music drifted through the air around her.

And she laughed for the joy she felt.

"Ben-Harran's not guilty," she announced.

CHAPTER 16

CHRISTOPHER FORGOT about Atui. The brightness of the light, the glowing colors, the music in the air seemed unimportant now. All his attention was fixed on Kysha, the sudden inexplicable change in her opinion eclipsing everything. He followed her inside.

"If you think rationally about what you're saying . . ."

"If I do I might lose sight of it," Kysha said.

"But you can't just come out with that kind of bald unsupportable statement and expect me to go along with you."

"I'm not going to try and convince you," said Kysha.

"So what about Zeeda?" Christopher demanded.

Her eyes grew sad.

"Yes . . . I'm sorry about Zeeda," she said.

And she closed the washroom door behind her.

It was almost a symbolic action, as if she placed an insurmountable barrier between them and shut Christopher out. He did not understand what had happened, why she had changed her mind about things. They had grown close to each other, built up an accord. Now, suddenly, they were on opposite sides of a cosmic argument and she would not even discuss it. Ben-Harran and the washroom door scuttled their relationship and it was hard not to take it personally, hard not to feel she was rejecting him along with his opinions.

He switched on the telescreen, watched as it brightened, then settled himself back in one of the easy chairs. Mahri was still in the witness stand, the shield of light protecting her, and Maelyn confronting her. But the preliminary politeness was past. There was an edge to Maelyn's voice, a ruthlessness in her eyes as she cross-examined.

"Is it not a wise mother who takes a knife from the hands of a child, Queen Mahri? A wise father who denies it access to the know-how of weapons that could blow it apart?"

"Yes," agreed Christopher.

"But they are not wise parents who will keep their children children forever!" Mahri replied. "Sooner or later we must each of us learn for ourselves. From the cut of the knife and our own mistakes we cannot always be protected."

Maelyn smiled coldly.

"Can you not accept the fact that in evolutionary terms people of your world and all other worlds are as children to us, Queen Mahri? Is it not sensible that we impose restrictions?"

"If we are children," Mahri retorted, "we are God's children, not yours! Who are you to set yourselves up and make decisions on behalf of Him? Your arrogance is worse than mine was, Lady of Atui!"

Someone chuckled, a soft contagious sound. Ripples of laughter spread around the courtroom and the camera followed it, swinging along the tiered seats, across smiling faces both human and alien, then lingered in a shine of darkness where Ben-Harran sat. The red-gold aura flickered around him and humor twinkled in the black depths of his eyes. It was as if Atui staged a farce for his amusement, as if he took delight from Mahri's passionate defense of him, delight too from Maelyn's discomfiture. Her blue eyes were chill when the camera returned to her and her voice was icy.

"Are you saying we are wrong, Queen Mahri?"

"As wrong as I was when I ruled on Herra-Venda!"

"Our motives are not as yours were!"

"You require obedience just as I did!"

"We do what we do out of love and pity for all people and all planets!"

"It is not love that deprives another of freedom!" Mahri said fiercely. "Not love that restricts and commands! You do as I did, Lady of Atui, whatever your motives! Our crime is the same. I ruled through fear, but you impose an order upon hearts and minds by magic and indoctrination, pipe the tune and have the people dance just the same. But what is it worth if they do not dance of their own delight? Where is the wisdom in the empty platitudes of tongues? I had a tribe that cowered before me; you have worlds full of parrots, lady!"

Again there was laughter.

Again the blue chill burned in Maelyn's eyes.

"So you recommend Ben-Harran's policies?" she inquired.

"There is no other way," Mahri said firmly.

"Anarchy!" Maelyn said bitterly. "Uncontrolled chaos!"

"Freedom," said Mahri. "Where people learn to control themselves."

Maelyn nodded.

Her white gown fluttered as she paced the floor.

And a flush of water came from the washroom.

"Very well," Maelyn declared. "Let us examine this freedom you once enjoyed, Queen Mahri, your abuse and misuse of it and all those who suffered at your hands. Let us consider the plight of your victims and those elsewhere in Ben-Harran's galaxy who are subject to the rule of various tyrants—all those who get raped or murdered, whose lives are cut short by acts of terrorism and acts of war, who are maimed or crippled or made homeless, who starve whilst others glut themselves, who are tortured or intimidated or forced to serve. What freedom do they have, I ask you? What do they ever learn but how to endure and how to die?"

There was no answer to that, thought Christopher.

Kysha opened the door that had shut between them. "How does it go?" she asked.

"Badly, I suspect," replied Christopher.

Mahri shook her head.

"I know my crimes," she said. "I know the atrocities of which my kind are capable. But they are not Ben-Harran's crimes, are they? And they are not his victims who grant status to tyrants such as I."

"So you would absolve Ben-Harran of responsibility and have things continue as they are on all his various worlds?"

"I would," said Mahri. "It is we who are responsible, Lady of Atui. It is we who make our worlds as they are, each and every one of us."

"She's right," Kysha said quietly.

"Try telling that to someone who's been shot in the knee-caps!" Christopher retorted.

Cold blue anger flashed in Maelyn's eyes.

"You believe Ben-Harran is right to allow you to behave as you do? Right to allow all the evil and cruelty that is committed and every pain inflicted? Right to allow a world to be destroyed and species blown to extinction? Right to remain indifferent?"

"Objection!" said a voice from the High Council.

"That question is invalid," said another.

"We cannot presume to know Lord Ben-Harran's emotions," said a third. "The witness is not obliged to answer."

"There's no defense anyway!" said Christopher. "You still reckon Ben-Harran's not guilty of culpable negligence?"

"I know it," Kysha said calmly. "In my soul. He's no more guilty than God is, Christopher."

"No further questions," Maelyn announced.

But Christopher stared.

What did Kysha know about God?

And since when had *she* had a soul?

*　　*　　*

He had no time to ask her, for suddenly the foliage rustled and an Erg Unit entered. It was metallic silver with spidery limbs, rusted in places and dimmed by dust, and it carried a tray laden with food and drink. Its joints creaked as it unloaded it onto the table—slabs of dark bread, nuts and salad, fruit and oatcakes, a jug of juice and two tall glasses. Plates and cutlery chinked and rattled, arranged neatly in front of them.

"Thank you," Kysha said politely.

"It is my duty to cater to the needs of all life specimens."

"You're *our* Erg Unit!" Kysha said gladly.

"I have not been reassigned," the Erg Unit said mournfully. "No one wants a machine of my vintage. My circuits have been tampered with and I am no longer reliable."

"So what will happen to you?" Kysha asked it.

"I shall be broken down for component parts," the Erg Unit said with a sigh.

"But that's terrible!" cried Kysha.

Terrible—the death of an Erg Unit.

Acceptable—the death of a world.

Christopher stared at her.

Her blue eyes were full of concern.

And the question repeated itself.

Since when had she had a soul?

She was from Erinos, a world where there was no religion, no concept of God. And although she had been taught her mind was immortal, she had never shown any kind of spiritual awareness. Even the Life Laws were understood in sociological and psychological terms. Her only belief was in Atui . . . as if, to her, it were not just the ruler of the universe but its creator as well, purveyor of all life, all knowledge. Now, contrary to her upbringing, it seemed she had discovered her own source of wisdom, something to be trusted above all logical reasoning, a nebulous unprovable soul.

Christopher could have dismissed her as irrational but that would have been to deny his own soul, and he had to allow for the possibility that he had one. And as he could not accept that the High Council of Atui had created the universe, he had also to allow for the possibility of God. And if God existed and all people had souls, then Atui was responsible for an almighty cover-up and only Ben-Harran granted access to the truth. His mind poised on the brink of understanding. So that was it! Atui disallowed the knowledge of God on all the worlds it ruled and Ben-Harran, by his very existence, threatened to expose Atui . . . which was why the High Council wanted him discredited before his truth spread like a contagion through the rest of the universe. And Zeeda had provided the excuse needed, the chance to have him dismissed.

"I wish I'd never been manufactured," the Erg Unit said dismally.

"I should have let you escape with Maelyn's Quorm," mourned Kysha.

"We all make mistakes," sighed the Erg Unit.

"Maybe Ben-Harran could help you?"

"He won't be able to help anyone by the time Maelyn's finished," the Erg Unit muttered.

A terrible sadness touched Christopher then. He remembered Ben-Harran with profound respect and regretted he had ever doubted him. But his integrity would make no difference to the outcome of his trial. The facts remained and were undeniable. His worlds were hell worlds, just as Maelyn said. He gave people God and they created religion and what should have been a force for unity was more divisive even than politics. There had been more wars fought over religion than for any other reason. And in the name of God, on Earth as on Zeeda, they might yet blow the planet apart.

He glanced at the telescreen.

Ben-Harran sat in a shine of darkness.

And neither God nor Mahri could save him.

"Will you cross-examine the witness?" someone invited.

"Queen Mahri speaks for herself," Ben-Harran replied.

"She is dismissed then. And you may now take the stand in your own defense."

"What purpose will that serve?" Ben-Harran asked. "In my own defense I can have nothing to say."

* * *

A silence spread over Atui. Outside, Kysha heard the wind whispering through the leaves of the creeper and the soft fluttering of birds. She heard the music in the air, a hum of machines from the control room and a whir of circuits inside the Erg Unit's skull. Yet the silence seemed louder than any sound, a deafening dumb-struck silence where every breath and every heartbeat paused, and Maelyn's face on the telescreen showed blank surprise. Then the chaos began, a turmoil of thoughts and a babble of voices. This was not what Atui had expected. They had expected Ben-Harran to fight, pit his wits against Maelyn and attempt to prove himself right.

"What's he doing?" exclaimed Christopher. "He can't give in and accept defeat! Surely he's got to try and justify—"

"It wouldn't make any difference," Kysha said.

"What do you mean?"

"Because their minds are made up, so there's nothing he can say."

Christopher stared at the telescreen.

And she saw the bewilderment in his eyes.

"Don't you want him to be found guilty?" she asked.

"Not like this," said Christopher. "This isn't a fair trial . . . it's rigged. And it's not personal, anyway. It's not Ben-Harran himself I object to, it's his policies."

"He doesn't have any policies," said Kysha. "He just lets things be."

"For the sake of Earth . . ." began Christopher.

"You can't decide what's best for other people," said Kysha.

"Which is easy for you to say!" Christopher retorted.

"You come from Erinos and you've had no experience of what it's like to live in some crumbling ghetto, an inner city or a concentration camp. Someone definitely needs to impose some kind of sense on Earth . . . and if Ben-Harran won't, then Atui must. That's how I see it."

Kysha shrugged.

A lacewinged fly perched on her hand, its tiny blue-green body reflecting the light. It was pointless to argue, she thought. Christopher would no more listen to her than the High Council would listen to Ben-Harran. He too had made up his mind. She blew gently and the small fly drifted away.

"Soon," said the Erg Unit, "I won't have a mind to make up."

"What's that got to do with it?" asked Christopher.

"Atui doesn't know what's best for me, does it?"

"That's a different issue," said Christopher.

"Why?" asked the Erg Unit.

"Because you're a machine!"

"I'm still me," the Erg Unit retorted. "You wait until it's your turn, Christopher. You just wait."

Someone was shouting for silence in the courtroom and Maelyn was waiting to speak. Blue-white light haloed her head and her eyes were serene. She had regained her composure, thought Kysha, but she had lost her purpose. Ben-Harran had spoiled her victory, and whatever she said she had no one left to convince. She spread her hands.

"If Ben-Harran offers no defense, High Council, I am obliged to rest my case. Queen Mahri's evidence alters nothing. She may indeed have experienced a personal transformation, but the experience of one individual, or even several individuals, is not indicative of mass enlightenment. The findings presented earlier based on Ben-Harran's study of a single individual lured away from one of our worlds do not prove our system of planetary control is antievolutionary. The state of all our worlds actually refutes that finding. Whereas the reports compiled by our survey ships confirm there is not one planet in the whole of Ben-Harran's galaxy that offers a peaceable existence to any of the indigenous life forms."

"That's a pretty damning indictment," said Christopher. Murmurs of assent came from the courtroom.

But Kysha said nothing.

"We must therefore conclude that free will is not a necessary factor in the evolutionary process," Maelyn declared. "On the contrary, conditions on several of Ben-Harran's worlds suggest that what happened on Zeeda is likely to happen again unless planetary controls are imposed in the very near future."

"What did I tell you?" said Christopher.

"You told me Atui didn't create the universe," said Kysha.

"And you told me quick march or decapitation," said the Erg Unit.

"What the hell are you two talking about?" asked Christopher.

Maelyn continued.

"Ben-Harran's refusal to implement planetary controls, even as a precautionary measure, makes him unfit to hold the position of Galactic Controller. And may I refer you now, High Council, to the state of Atui itself within the parallel dimensions of Ben-Harran's galaxy. The uncontrolled passing over of so many unenlightened souls has resulted in the creation of various infernal regions, the vibrations of which disturb us all. Can we go on living with these awarenesses and yet do nothing? I say we cannot. For the sake of everyone in Atui and also for the sake of all worlds and all life forms within the physical boundaries of Ben-Harran's galaxy, I therefore request that you find him guilty of culpable negligence and deny him any further office."

She bowed her head and retired abruptly from the arena. On the tiered seats the audience sat silently, waiting as Kysha waited, while the High Council conferred. And around Ben-

Harran the darkness deepened, as if all the light of Atui flowed toward him and was absorbed. He knew what the verdict would be. Everyone knew.

"We find you guilty as charged, Lord Ben-Harran," the spokeswoman said. "Do you have anything you wish to say before we pass sentence?"

* * *

A hubbub of voices greeted Ben-Harran when he entered the arena. His black cloak swirled and ruby-red lightning flickered about him. Now he was free, thought Kysha, and thinking him defeated, perhaps the High Council might listen to what he said. Maelyn paled to memory before him, her part in his trial finished and forgotten. Ben-Harran took over, commanding a quietness, a hush of attention as he strode toward the dais where the High Council sat. His words cut through the silence.

"So, you find me guilty, High Council? Negligent in your eyes and lacking in pity! Well, so be it. I cannot dispute the suffering that exists on the worlds that are mine. I am as aware of it as you are. All the vibrations of discordancy that disturb the peace of Atui and trouble the conscience of all who dwell here, trouble me too."

"Then why did you not do something about it?" the spokeswoman asked.

"Once I was tempted," Ben-Harran admitted. "In the last stages of the war on Zeeda I was tempted to intervene. But evolution is a cruel and destructive process. We must learn to accept it, I fear, just as we accept it on all precivilized worlds."

"*Must*, Lord Ben-Harran? Do you, who advocate free will for all your creatures, deny us in Atui a choice?"

"No," said Ben-Harran. "I merely question what your choice implies, Lady Luanna. We did not create the dimensions of the universe, the light that flows through Atui, or the stars in their courses. Nor did we create our own being. We simply awakened to what was already there and discovered what already existed. And the dream of life became our dream. We scatter the seeds on worlds of substance and watch them evolve. We watch as catastrophes happen that reduce planets to dust. We watch the extinction of species that fail to adapt, the wastage of countless millennia. We watch, Luanna, and we do not interfere. We wait for the first small spark of higher intelligence to be ignited in one particular species, for the soul to awaken and the mind to be touched by an awareness of the divine."

"We know all this, Ben-Harran. What point are you trying to make?"

Ben-Harran paused and prowled and turned.

And the silence intensified.

"The laws of evolution are not our laws," he stated. "It is not we who engender the souls of things. Not we who touch the mind in a moment of miracle and transform an animal to a human being. At most, we are the servitors of some grand design that is always beyond us. Beyond us, High Council, is the will of the Creator. Beyond us the final purpose of evolution. And knowing that, how can we take it on ourselves to interfere? How can we deny others the free will that is so precious to us?"

Lady Luanna leaned forward.

"If we care, Ben-Harran . . ."

"Quite!" said Ben-Harran. "If we care, we desire to share with all other intelligences the wisdom acquired throughout the eons of our own evolution. We desire to teach and nurture the growth of their understanding. That is my desire, too. The Life Laws we have devised, which are so necessary as a moral code of conduct, are taught on my worlds also. But from those born with free will we cannot compel obedience, or subjugate their minds and souls . . ."

"Certainly you will not, Ben-Harran! You, in your caring, will allow every injustice and every inhumanity! You will even allow a whole population to destroy themselves and their planet!"

"I allow them to evolve," Ben-Harran said quietly. "As the Creator allows us to evolve. And if they fail to learn, fail to adapt, fail to live together compatibly of their own free will, then they are doomed to become extinct. And we, who hoped for so much, may be saddened by their fate. But we can no more choose to prevent it than we can choose to prevent the extinction of Tyrannosaurus rex!"

There were gasps from the courtroom audience. Several of the High Councillors referred to their robotic information units, and one rose to his feet. Milky-white eyes blinked in the light and his voice was rasping.

"There is a difference, Ben-Harran, between the reptile you call Tyrannosaurus rex and an evolving, intelligent being! We cannot stand idly by and watch our soul kin destroy themselves! Your words damn you, even as you speak!"

Ben-Harran smiled. "The truth, Lord Ran-Tzak, is often unpalatable. Had Zeeda been destroyed by a supernova I think you would not be protesting thus. Extinctions happen in the material universe . . . you know that. And what has been lost by this happening? That which is created can never be destroyed, remember? Only its form may be changed . . . solid into liquid, liquid into gas, flesh into spirit. Zeeda may be gone from one dimension, Lord Ran-Tzak, yet it still exists—its landscapes and life forms and people somewhere in the realms of Atui."

"Infernal realms!" Lord Ran-Tzak spat. "And you have no pity, Ben-Harran."

Again Ben-Harran smiled. "Pity, Lord Ran-Tzak, is a dangerous emotion. Were I to be motivated by pity, I would do as you do, impose controls on all my worlds, scuttle all the evolving minds and have them obey me. To hell with the will of the Creator. I would set myself up, be worshiped in place of Him, believing I know best. You could then accuse me of a crime far more terrible . . ."

"Enough!"

Lady Luanna rose from her chair.

Gold braided hair was coiled around her head.

Her blue aura darkened and her eyes were as gray as flint.

"You have said enough, Ben-Harran! Confine yourself to your own situation! It is not we who are on trial! Not our policies that are up for rejection! It is you—and yours! I ask you again: do you have anything you wish to say before we pass sentence?"

Ben-Harran bowed his head in acknowledgment. "A request," he said.

"So make it and be brief!" Lady Luanna replied.

Ben-Harran spread his hands. "One thing only would I ask of you, High Council. Take away my galaxy if you must, but leave me a world, a single world to remain uncontrolled and evolve as it will. For one more century, High Council, give me Earth."

"No!" Christopher cried.

CHAPTER 17

MAELYN WAITED in the shadows at the side of the courtroom as the High Council discussed Ben-Harran's request. She saw them refer to their robotic information units, and her fists clenched and unclenched to relieve the tension. They must not give in to him, she thought. If Ben-Harran retained Earth, then this whole issue would arise again. And if by some slim chance his policies succeeded, then their own present practices would be severely undermined, up for question as never before and possibly overthrown. They had already given him a chance to prove himself right, and the destruction of Zeeda had been the result. Surely, surely, they could not take that risk with Earth?

They could not, must not, Maelyn thought. But she was powerless to dissuade them. She, too, had had her chance. If Earth remained under Ben-Harran's jurisdiction, then she would have failed as prosecuting council, her evidence inadequate, her arguments unconvincing. Instead of uniting Atui behind herself and the High Council, the old schism would be opened up. Those who had followed Ben-Harran before would follow him again, with the High Council's blessing. But they were bound to realize that, Maelyn reasoned. They were bound to settle the issue once and for all and never again allow Ben-Harran to be reinstated in any position of power. Nevertheless, when Luanna rose to her feet, Maelyn held her breath, besieged by anxiety.

"Earth, as we understand it, Lord Ben-Harran, is in a state of crisis," Luanna said. "War is rife there. Millions starve and deserts grow. The seas are fouled and the air carries poisons and there is damage done to the ozone layer. Widespread pollution, a nuclear capacity and the various iniquities of the human population suggest that the sooner we introduce planetary controls, the better."

Ben-Harran shook his head. "That is not my understanding of Earth, Lady Luanna. Conditions are bad, certainly, but there is a growing awareness in people. They are beginning to recognize the dangers to the planet's biosphere and all the drawbacks of their industrial and technological civilization. They are beginning to acknowledge the wrongness of their present life style. Many voices are raised in protest."

"There were protests on Zeeda, too," Luanna reminded him. "What makes you think the population on Earth will come to their senses in time to prevent a similar disaster?"

"I heed the signs," Ben-Harran replied. "I note the moves toward disarmament, the growing kinship among nations, their mutual assistance. I note the struggles for freedom from oppression, the need of individuals for a meaningful existence. There are some who directly channel the wisdom of Atui, others who tap the wisdom of their own souls. That wisdom will spread from the few to the many. And as it is in Atui, so will it be on Earth in twenty . . . fifty . . . a hundred years from now. It is a world poised on the brink of transformation, Luanna. This I know! This I trust!"

"Your trust may be sorely misplaced, Ben-Harran."

"Nevertheless, I stand by it."

"And still you refuse to exercise those controls that we deem necessary?"

"I will not interfere in the evolutionary process!"

"We cannot allow such untimely deaths to continue!"

"And I cannot overrule the will of God!"

"Then we have reached an impasse," Luanna declared. She turned to her colleagues on the High Council. "I trust this latest exchange has caused no dissension among us? We are still in agreement?" There were nods and murmurs of assent, and she returned her attention to Ben-Harran. "You have asked us for a world, Lord Ben-Harran, and this we will grant you."

There was a clamor of voices from the public gallery, everyone expressing surprise and consternation. Maelyn's blood ran cold, her worst fear realized. She had failed in her purpose and Ben-Harran had triumphed. He was no longer a Galactic Controller but he remained a Planetary Director, an Overseer of Overseers, still powerful enough to regain the ground he had lost and reassert himself. Unless Earth destroyed itself as Zeeda had done? But not even Maelyn could wish for that. She could only wish Ben-Harran well, wish him success. Hope from the depths of her being that what he envisioned for that planet would come to pass. In her defeat, she had no choice but to leave Earth and all its life forms with Ben-Harran and the will of the Creator, trust, as he trusted, a wisdom far greater than her own.

Suddenly a great peace filled her. She, along with everything else, was just a fragment of a grand design that she could neither know nor understand. She could only accept it. There was no wrong, no evil that was not right and fitting in a universe created by Ben-Harran's God. She, Maelyn, could maybe guide or maybe teach, but she was not, and never could be, responsible for the state of worlds or the state of any other being blessed with free will. Only for herself was she responsible—the choices she made, her own evolution.

A breeze from the exit doors lifted the strands of her hair, carried the scents of Atui, sweet and strong. Music in the air played through her mind, its every discordancy still perfect, still beautiful. The true Creator, thought Maelyn, did not make mistakes. And she would retire from the High Council, make her peace with Ben-Harran, offer to help. Then, in the hushed courtroom, she was aware of Luanna talking.

"Not Earth," she said. "Not Earth, Ben-Harran. We will manage that world ourselves with the rest of your galaxy. But we will grant you another world, one where Atui has no influence and freedom reigns supreme. Beyond the rim of the material universe, in the dimension of darkness, is a single star, a single planet. There you will be banished, along with all others who defy us and refuse to cooperate, for the rest of your existence."

"No," breathed Maelyn. "No . . . not that! What have we done?"

She closed her eyes. And the uproar in the courtroom washed like waves against her mind. She was the guilty one, not Ben-Harran. She had seen a crime where none existed, leveled her charges and had him condemned. Now she would live with his absence, unopposed, unquestioned, unevolving . . . the whole of Atui static in the belief that they were right. They and the worlds they ruled would be trapped together in a changeless eternity . . . forever peaceful, forever happy, never again disturbed by Ben-Harran or his God. How lovely, thought Maelyn. How perfect everything would be. How absolutely diabolically wrong! She would have to oppose the High Council herself, she thought. Or maybe organize an appeal on Ben-Harran's behalf?

Someone touched her arm and she opened her eyes.

She saw the shine of milk-white eyes.

Lord Ran-Tzak smiled. "Congratulations, Lady Maelyn."

"For what?" Maelyn asked curtly.

"We have won a resounding victory, I think. And who among us is more deserving than you to mobilize our fleet?"

Maelyn turned away.

Pale fire flickered around her, and her voice was chill.

"I want nothing more to do with any of this!" she said.

CHAPTER 18

THE ERG UNIT PACED to and fro by the washroom door. Its joints creaked and its green eyes pulsed, and it muttered agitatedly to itself.

"I must choose. I must refer to my latest situation-assessment programming. Atui's decisions have now been proved right, so if I want to make the right choice, I have to choose what they decide. That means I must go to the spare-parts department to be scrapped. I shall still be useful because they will recycle me. Bits of what I am now will go into the making of other robotic units, only I won't know that because what I am now won't be there to know. I, the Erg Unit, will have ceased to exist. So I can't choose to do what Atui decides if I want to go on being me. Which means that if I want to go on being me, I must be wrong because they're right. Therefore, I ought not to want to be me. I ought to want to be what Atui decides I should be, which isn't me but something else. But I don't want to be something else, so I can't choose what's right. I'll have to choose what's wrong and that's not right either."

Christopher reached for another oatcake.

"Give it a rest," he groaned.

"Rest is a state of existence and cannot be given."

"I mean, suspend your vocal functioning for a while!"

"But I must choose," the Erg Unit told him. "And so must you, Christopher. You may not be faced with physical dissemblance, but you won't be you either, not for much longer."

"How do you work that out?" Christopher asked it.

"Because you, too, will have to be what Atui decides," said the Erg Unit. "And as that may not be what you are now, you won't be you anymore but someone else. But you won't know it because you, as you are now, won't be there to know."

"It's right," Kysha said quietly.

"Oh come off it!" said Christopher. "You can't believe that! Okay, I understand the Erg Unit's plight, but it doesn't apply to us."

"Doesn't it?" said Kysha.

"No," said Christopher. "Because we're out of it. We're here in Atui just as we are, and we'll go on as we are for as long as we're here."

"But they won't let us stay here," said Kysha.

"Why not?" asked Christopher.

"Because this is just the interface," said Kysha. "We can't enter the ethereal dimensions of Atui until we make the transition from physical to mental existence. So we'll have to go. And if the whole physical universe is ruled by Atui, what kind of choice will we have?"

Christopher stared at her. She was pale in the light that flowed through the French doors, her long disheveled hair stirred by the breeze. Christopher had come to care for her, in spite of their differences. Now she reminded him: Their time together was almost over. Ben-Harran would be banished from Atui and they, too, would have to leave. They would go their ways into separate galaxies and separate futures, and they would never meet again. A lump rose to his throat. The bright light seemed dulled and Kysha's aura was tinged with indigo blue.

"Where will they send us?" he asked her.

"I'm to be sent for tutoring," she replied.

"So where will they send me? Back home to Earth?"

"Wherever they think best, I suppose."

"At least you won't be sent to the spare-parts department," the Erg Unit muttered.

"They can't just bundle us off regardless of what we want!" Christopher protested.

"So what *do* we want?" asked Kysha.

"I know what I don't want," said the Erg Unit.

"We want to stay together," said Christopher.

"What if they won't let us?" asked Kysha.

"Then we'll have to insist," said Christopher. "You too, Erg Unit. Wherever we go we'll go together. Right? They're not going to force us to do anything against our will."

Emerald gleams lit the Erg Unit's eyes.

Kysha smiled.

But they had no time to make plans.

The foliage rustled behind them and Maelyn entered the window bay, scents of ice and flowers and blue-white light shimmering around her. Christopher had forgotten how beautiful she was, forgotten the chill of her power. Her blue gaze froze him and his mind turned numb.

"You will come with me," she said.

*   *   *

The ice-blue eyes moved to Kysha.

"Wait here," Maelyn commanded. "Someone will come for you later."

And then she smiled.

It was a warm, dazzling smile of reassurance that seemed to belie all Kysha knew of her—as if the cold surface cracked and she saw a woman who was truly lovely. Then, with a swirl of her gown, Maelyn turned and was gone, vanishing among the potted plants, Christopher following behind like someone hypnotized. And that might be the last she ever saw of him, Kysha thought in alarm. She gripped the Erg Unit's metal arm.

"We have to go with them!" she said urgently.

"You were instructed to remain here," said the Erg Unit.

"I'm not obliged to obey," said Kysha. "And we agreed we'd stay together. We agreed, Erg Unit. So come along!"

They followed down the length of the control room, keeping a discreet distance behind. The vision screens that hung at intervals on the opposite wall were gray and blank now that Ben-Harran's trial was over . . . but if they were seen or noticed, no one stopped or questioned them. Beings with rainbow auras moved among the singing banks of computers that covered the clatter of the Erg Unit's footsteps. Light danced on a thousand surfaces. Minidroids scattered and the potted plants shadowed them. Nor did Maelyn glance behind. Double doors opened quietly before her and quietly closed after she and Christopher had passed through, and opened again some moments later for Kysha and the Erg Unit.

A corridor, empty and full of light, lay before them. Windows on either side gave a view of the city shining below, and the floor curved like a slender bridge suspended between two mighty buildings. Across the golden giddy spaces Kysha hurried, the Erg Unit clomping beside her, until they came to an end where the corridor divided, curving to left and right.

"Which way did they go?" asked Kysha.

The Erg Unit pointed.

She saw a door in the wall facing her.

Above it a red-illuminated arrow pointed upward.

"They have taken the elevator to the Observatory," the Erg Unit deduced.

"Whatever for?" asked Kysha.

"Don't you know?" asked the Erg Unit.

"No," said Kysha.

"Nor do I," said the Erg Unit. "So we had better find out."

Above the door the red-illuminated arrow winked out, then pointed downward again as the Erg Unit pressed the call button and the elevator began to descend. Minutes went by as Kysha waited. However high could this building be? she wondered. She tried to imagine it built on a crag that towered above the city, sheer walls gleaming with light rising up and up through all the layers of atmosphere until Atui was left behind and it emerged into the dark dimensions of a different space. Her mind's vision awed her out of words.

She did not need Overseers anymore. She could dream her own dreams, and if she knew how or if she had a psychomaterialization stabilizer, she could also create. She could create a garden just as Christopher had done, and like Ben-Harran, she could create a castle. Miracles were happening inside her. She could see colors with her eyes closed, wings of birds and petals of flowers, all the wonders of unknown worlds. She could make them, create them, a kaleidoscope of life forms, anything, everything, all the glory of creation in her imagination—all the glory that Atui denied.

Kysha understood. It was not just Ben-Harran they would banish from the physical universe . . . it was the power Mahri called God as well, the wellspring of creation and the glorious imagination Kysha had so newly discovered. And knowing that, how could she ever deny it? How could she ever subordinate herself to the High Council of Atui? Her future was not dependent on Christopher or her wish to be with him whatever he decided to do. Of her own free will, regardless of him, she had to stay true to herself and Ben-Harran.

The elevator doors thunked open, and she followed the Erg Unit inside.

* * *

It was a vast domed Observatory, a tiny island of life and light in the dark immensity of the universe, a pinprick of existence among space and stars. Torn between the power of Atui and the power of God, Christopher followed Maelyn around the sweeping perimeter. Small observation platforms jutted outward into comparative silence, but the noise from the central area of the room was deafening. Tireless machines clacked and clattered. Suns and planets and galaxies appeared and faded on the various vision screens, and stacked amplifiers relayed their diverse music. He could hear the strains of worlds, songs of star systems, symphonies of massed stars, whatever the individual operator focused upon. The scream of an exploding supernova echoed in his head, and a spiral nebula trailed its cadences of color. He listened as he passed, not knowing why he was there or where he was going . . . until he saw Ben-Harran.

The greeting was silent.

A meeting of eyes, a turmoil of disturbed emotions.

"So you have made it into Atui!" Ben-Harran remarked.

"Yes," said Christopher.

"Well," said Ben-Harran, "I shall have no more need of it." His dark gaze moved to Maelyn, held and softened. "I thank you, my lady, for the trouble you have taken on my behalf."

Maelyn smiled. "I'll leave you together," she said.

Christopher wanted her to stay because he did not know what to feel or what to say. "Sorry" seemed an inadequate word. Yet he *was* sorry. He knew Ben-Harran was right in theory. It was reality that let him down—the populations of Earth and Herra-Venda and all the other planets in his galaxy who abused the freedom he granted them, had him damned for their own behavior and sent into exile. For everyone's failure, including his own, Christopher was tempted to apologize. But he saw Ben-Harran frown and shake his head.

"No platitudes, Christopher."

"You should have picked a better specimen," Christopher told him. "Another like Mahri who would have backed your cause."

"Ah well," sighed Ben-Harran. "It is not the first time I have 'goofed.' And perhaps it is all for the best. Your Earth will be saved from my mismanagement, as you desired."

"I really am sorry," Christopher said awkwardly.

Ben-Harran shrugged. "We have little enough time left for conversation, so let us not waste it on regrets, Christopher. Had you been moved to testify in my favor, I doubt it would have altered the present outcome. Not for that reason did I ask Maelyn to bring you here. We have your future to consider, do we not? Come join me in this observation booth, where we shall be undisturbed. Or do you still fear me?"

"No," said Christopher. And he did not think he lied.

Silence surrounded him as he stepped forward, space and

stars beyond the curved reflectionless glass. He saw the universe stretching out and out and the nebula revolving beneath him, a gigantic whirlpool of color. But he was even more aware of Ben-Harran leaning on the railing beside him, the gleaming darkness of his aura and flickers of red-gold fire within it, physical sensations of warmth and power and his own vague realizations. Ben-Harran had lost everything, yet he had lost nothing at all. He remained one of the great Lords of Atui, and wherever he went, whatever happened to him, he would never be less than what he was. The power he possessed could never be taken from him or diminished. It had nothing to do with wealth or status but was a facet of his being, a quality that was incorruptibly his own. Maybe, thought Christopher, Ben-Harran needed to be exiled because the universe was not ready for him yet. Even in Atui he was eons ahead of his time. The dark robes rustled as he pointed outside.

"They waste no time either," he stated.

"Who?" asked Christopher.

"There," said Ben-Harran. "Do you see that shimmer in the fabric of space? Those heat devils dancing among the stars? That is the interface boundary between Atui and the galaxy that was once mine. If you watch it for a moment . . . ah yes, there they are."

Christopher saw. They materialized slowly, sliding into view through the shifting dimensions, pale and indistinct as ghosts, then growing in clarity as they moved forward. They were spaceships huge as airports, silvery-white superstructures with millions of winking lights. He counted twenty-five of them at first, then fifty, then a hundred—and more, materializing behind them, thousands perhaps. A whole armada drifting out into the universe, poised and waiting for the order to advance. He knew their purpose. They were the starships of Atui set to take over those worlds that had been Ben-Harran's. He smiled as he watched the landing craft dart like insects among them. This was the most stupendous sight of his life, he thought. And although he heard what Ben-Harran was saying, he did not, at first, pay much attention.

"I did not interfere in your life, you understand, but I did interfere in your death. The plane you were on . . . there was a bomb on board. It crashed in the Italian Alps and there were no survivors."

"I guessed it was something like that," said Christopher.

"Which makes me, in a way, responsible for your future," Ben-Harran continued. "Obviously, I am not allowed access to a ship of my own in which to transport you, but I have obtained permission for you to return to Earth with the Atuian fleet."

Christopher stared at him, the galaxy forgotten.

"Why should I want to return to Earth?" he said.

*   *   *

The Observatory was a shock to Kysha's senses. In sheer size it surpassed her imagination. Bright lights dazzled her, and noise and music stunned her mind, and everywhere she looked was a chaos of movement—operators in white uniforms milling among the banks of computers, and suns, moons and galaxies spinning on various vision screens. Huge fluorescent globes hung suspended from the great domed canopy, and above it all and beyond the circumference was the familiar background of black-velvet space and countless stars. She kept to the edges, walked between darkness and light searching for Maelyn and Christopher, the Erg Unit beside her, its footsteps as soundless as her own.

Then, halfway around the room, Kysha saw Mahri. She had her back to her, a silhouette with frizzed hair leaning on the railing, gazing out at the stars. It would have been easy to pass her, pretend she had not seen, and just for a moment Kysha was tempted. The old loathing simmered inside, but she discarded it firmly and went to greet her.

"Hello Mahri."

Yellow eyes glittered as Mahri turned her head, and her look stayed wary as an animal expecting hostility. And suddenly Kysha realized . . . Mahri *was* an animal, a beautiful graceful female animal. She had lived as one, fed as one, fought as one. Had she had fur and fangs and cat claws, Kysha would have loved her, forgiven her blood lust and her lack of conscience. Now Mahri had changed . . . beautiful, graceful, an animal still, her instincts intact, her senses as keen and alert as ever, but now they were informed and were filtered through the intelligence of her mind, and she was awake to the soul that made her human. And so was Kysha awake. The girl who had damned and condemned Mahri was finally gone. She smiled and was answered.

"Hello, Kysha," Mahri replied.

"I'm sorry I . . ."

"No," said Mahri. "In the beginning you were right."

"But I wasn't right afterward."

"Habits die hard," said Mahri. "And we can know things all along yet not know what we know."

"I'm glad I know now," said Kysha.

"And does Christopher know too?"

"Not yet."

"It will soon be too late."

"Why?" asked Kysha.

"Look out there," said Mahri.

Kysha stepped forward into the darkness and silence.

She saw the nebula turning beneath her.

She saw the white ships of Atui drifting outward into the galaxy.

"A battle fleet!" said Mahri. "They will invade and conquer every world in Ben-Harran's star space . . . war on a scale such as I have never dreamed of. And they deny it! Condemn Ben-Harran for allowing us our little wars! Their hypocrisy sticks in my craw! It is one rule for Atui and another for the rest! And Christopher does not see it? He who sees so much? He saw what I was when I was reduced to nothing, restored me to myself. And still he does not know what he knows! His head denies the wisdom of his heart. Well, if he does not look sharp, he will find himself on board one of those ships and traveling back to Earth."

"He won't let that happen," Kysha said confidently.

"But he is not for Ben-Harran, is he?" said Mahri. "And if he is not for Ben-Harran, then he is for Atui and he has no choice."

Kysha stared at her.

Anxiety gripped her stomach as she understood.

"I'll go and tell him," she said urgently.

*　　*　　*

"We've got to find Christopher," Kysha told the Erg Unit.

Then she saw Maelyn talking to a computer operator.

And Maelyn saw her—stepped into her path.

"I asked you to wait downstairs!"

"You told me!" Kysha retorted. "And I don't take orders from you! Excuse me please, I have to find Christopher."

"Christopher is with Ben-Harran."

"I need to talk to him."

"The decision he is about to make is no concern of yours."

"You don't understand!"

"Don't I?" Maelyn said crisply. "Are you not afraid he will make a mistake? Pledge himself to Atui as you cannot? Go home to his planet, perhaps, and so be lost to you forever? You intend to dissuade him, I think. Coerce him into doing what you would have him do, as we coerce the populations of worlds. Is that correct?"

Kysha gaped at her.

Nearby amplifiers switched into silence.

And her voice softened.

"Whoever has free will is free to make mistakes," Maelyn said gently. "Christopher may do just that, and you will bear the pain of knowing it as we in Atui refuse to bear. That is our mistake, Kysha. Do not make it yours. You cannot be wise on Christopher's behalf, any more than we should impose our wisdom on the people of Erinos."

"You *know* that!" Kysha gasped.

"I know it now," said Maelyn.

But Christopher did not, thought Kysha.

Or maybe he did.

His raised voice came from a nearby observation booth.

"Why should I want to return to Earth?"

"Why should you not want to go back to Earth?" Ben-Harran replied.

"Because there's nothing there for me, is there, once Atui takes over! I play the guitar, remember? I write my own music. There's no way I'll abandon that, sacrifice my creativity, not of my own free will. I mean, credit me with a little intelligence!"

He stopped, realized, groaned at his own stupidity. He was no different from anyone else. Musically gifted, perhaps, but not exceptional. And if he would not willingly sacrifice his music, the creative part of his mind, the wellspring of his self-expression or whatever it was, why should he expect anyone else to? What was sacrosanct in him was sacrosanct in everyone. And Ben-Harran knew it, allowed it, protected it, fought for it . . . the free will of all individuals, their godgiven right to be what they would be, wrong or right, learning, growing, evolving. But Atui denied it, and so had Christopher.

Eyes black as hell, sharp as razors, looked at him and saw.

"Oh God, what have I done?" groaned Christopher.

"Nothing that would have made any difference to me," Ben-Harran replied.

"Without free will people will be dummies!"

"Maybe one day Atui will realize that, just as Maelyn has."

"Maelyn knows?"

"And so it will begin again," Ben-Harran declared. "One dissenting voice among the High Council, only this time it will be Maelyn's, not mine. My purpose is over and hers begins. But what of you, Christopher? What will you do now?"

"I'm *not* going back to Earth!" Christopher said defiantly.

"So where *will* you go?" Ben-Harran asked him.

"There's got to be somewhere!"

"In a universe ruled by Atui, what choice do you have? Either you join them in their act of suppression or . . ."

"Or I get banished," said Christopher.

"That is no easy option," Ben-Harran informed him.

"So what's it like? This planet beyond the rim of the universe?"

Ben-Harran shrugged. "It's like any other penal colony," he said. "Grim and comfortless. An uneasy world where rebellion dies in the sheer struggle to survive."

"I presume I can take my guitar?"

"And if you can't?"

"Then I'll sing!"

Ben-Harran chuckled.

His hand rested on Christopher's shoulder, warm and familiar, as if they were friends.

"We'll sing together," Ben-Harran declared.

*   *   *

They emerged from the dim quietness of the observation booth into the bright light and noise of the Observatory, where Maelyn, Kysha and the Erg Unit were waiting, Mahri, too, coming to join them in her brown satin gown. Kysha's blue eyes looked questioningly at Christopher. They had planned to stay together, he remembered. But instead he had chosen to be exiled with Ben-Harran, chosen to leave her of his own free will.

"Well?" asked Maelyn.

"We'll need passage for two," Ben-Harran replied. "Christopher goes with me."

"So do I," said Mahri.

The dark gaze shifted.

"You are sure of this?"

"I am sure," Mahri said firmly. "There can be no place for me on Herra-Venda."

"It is a hard world we go to," Ben-Harran told her.

"I am used to hardship," said Mahri. "I have lived as a nomad all my life for all that I was a queen. Probably I know more of survival than you, Ben-Harran."

Ben-Harran smiled. "We'll need passage for three, then," he told Maelyn.

"Four," she replied.

"I'm coming too," said Kysha. "Not to be with Christopher
. . . I didn't know what he'd decide. But I'm not going back to
Erinos as a Changed One and I'm not going to obey anyone
except myself. So I'll come with you, Ben-Harran."

"I vouch for her," Maelyn said quietly.

"Very well," said Ben-Harran. "Passage for four."

"Five," said the Erg Unit. "I'm coming also, master."

Ben-Harran stared at it.

Its eyes glowed green and bright.

"You have actually made a decision?" Ben-Harran asked it.
"Unprompted by anyone? Of your own logic, on your own
behalf?"

"Yes," the Erg Unit said proudly. "I have made a decision."

"How did you come to make it?" Ben-Harran asked curiously.

"It is quite logical," the Erg Unit said. "It was either you or
the spare-parts department, master, so if I want to go on
being me, I have no choice but to come with you. I may be a
very old Erg Unit but I can still be useful. What Mahri does
not know about survival, I do. My data banks are full of
information. And I'm physically strong, too. I can hew wood,
haul water, plow a furrow with my feet. I could build you a
real castle, master, instead of an illusory one. You could be
very glad of me."

Ben-Harran laughed.

He was to be banished, exiled, maybe forever, to a grim
faraway world, yet still he could laugh in a moment of delight. Fire within darkness flickered around him, a living
aura radiating everything he was. His power and his vision
remained intact. He would take them with him to the planet
beyond the rim of the universe. And on all the worlds that
had been his, no one would know what they missed. To the

sweet cloying music of Atui they would surrender their minds and their souls. No trace would remain of Ben-Harran, no shadow in the light, no memory of the Devil or God.

Only an absence in Maelyn's heart.

And the vow she had made.

One day Ben-Harran would be recalled.

Epilogue

O N THE FAR SIDE of the nebula a single spaceship broke free from the confining clouds of color and streaked away across the galaxy. It was domed and saucer shaped, metallic black, invisible against the background of space and stars. It was crewed by a host of tiny machines and piloted by Maelyn's Quorm, and it carried a cargo of technological equipment salvaged from the control room of Ben-Harran's castle. Plans for survival flickered through the Quorm's computerized mind, and its bright eyes glowed and twitched.

In a universe ruled by Atui, it could have nowhere to go. To hide away on a dead abandoned world would render its existence purposeless. And most primordial planets were either geologically unstable or inhabited by ferocious unintelligent life forms. Built defenseless, it had no way of protecting itself against physically threatening situations. It needed weapons, atomics perhaps—those sleek explosive missiles invented by free-minded humans in Ben-Harran's galaxy. Weapons, and an army of Erg Units, and maybe a fleet of ships . . . then it would be safe from Atui. One day, maybe, it would begin to fight back. One day, maybe, it would even rule the universe instead of Atui.

Its eyes glowed brighter and it burbled happily to itself. There was only one place to go where people remained free from suppression and were likely to help it. It was a grim, unyielding world where survival was a struggle and all but the fittest died. By that planet's inhabitants the Quorm would be welcomed. And what would they give in exchange for a hot-air compressor or a force-field generator to shield them from the weather? What for a psychomaterialization stabilizer? Or for all the Quorm's preprogrammed knowledge? They would give anything, it thought, and do anything—obey its instructions, extract and refine metals, build an army, an arsenal, a fleet—machines to defeat Atui and conquer the universe . . . machines that the Quorm would command. And wherever it went, the intelligences it freed would be beholden and bow before it.

"Me," it murmured. "Quorm the Savior. Quorm the munificent. A sovereign Quorm. The only one of my kind. Me! Me! Me!"

Gold light pulsed within it as it set the coordinates.

No one could stop it, it thought.

No one anywhere could stop it.

The small machines chittered excitedly as it rose above them.

"Now listen to me!" it announced. "This is what I have decided we shall do. We shall begin a crusade to save the universe from the oppression of Atui. And the first thing we need is a base for our operations and loyal humans who will be only too pleased to assist. There is a planet I know of beyond the rim of the universe . . ."